The Gastrothief

STEVE HIGGS

Contents

Prologue

"Incompetent!" The Earl slammed his pudgy hand down, striking the surface of his table with enough force to make the cutlery and crockery jump. The pepper grinder wobbled before toppling.

The Earl's hand hurt, a fact he refused to show as he glared at the three men standing opposite.

"Incompetent?" Blake repeated. He'd had more than enough of the gluttonous peer and his demands. It just wasn't worth the pay. "How about if you show us how it's done, you fat git?"

Earl Bacon's rage was at boiling point anyway, being spoken back to by an underling, a mere hired skivvy ...

"How dare you!" he spat, attempting to rise from his chair. His perfectly cooked Beef Wellington was going cold, another fact fuelling his rage.

Blake wanted to choke the life out of the miserable, entitled tub of lard, but judged his colleagues were more than likely to kill him if he tried. They would do almost anything for the Earl simply because he threw money around like it was confetti.

Instead, he picked an option he wished he'd taken weeks ago: he walked out.

"Where the devil do you think you are going?" Earl Bacon bellowed. "Get back here!"

Blake didn't even bother to look over his shoulder.

"That's it then," the Earl spat at the departing man's back. "You're out! Do you hear? You're out! Your colleagues will be saved, but you won't. Come crawling back when the world outside crumbles and fails, but you won't get in!"

The two men Blake came in with hadn't moved and were yet to respond to their colleague's outburst. The Earl's crazy rantings were nothing new. He was unshakably convinced the world was about to end in a spectacular fashion. Overpopulation, pollution, goodness knows what else. He had detailed theories and papers from people he referred to as leading scientists.

Wayne and Boris didn't believe a word of his paranoid nonsense, but saw no need to rock the boat. The Earl paid them far more than their efforts were worth and he was yelling at them now because they had failed to achieve a goal that both believed was nigh impossible.

Find Albert Smith.

Find one man.

Ordinarily that might not be too hard, but the nation's police were also looking for him and they hadn't managed to locate him in more than a week. Wayne and Boris hadn't even tried. Each day they would tell their boss all about what they had done and where they had gone, but it was all lies. Assigned to scour the country and find the old man, they moved around sure enough, but spent their time taking leisurely pub lunches and reading the *Racing Post* for the day's top tips.

The Earl was increasingly impatient, but they didn't care.

When the sound of Blake's receding footsteps faded to nothing, Wayne said, "We will increase our efforts, Sir. He cannot hide forever."

Earl Bacon narrowed his eyes at the two men.

"Don't bother."

Startled because it was the last thing they expected to hear, both men stared back at the Earl with slack-jawed expressions.

"I'm sorry, Sir," Boris needed to check his understanding. "You're telling us to stop looking for Albert Smith?"

"Yes." The Earl sliced a piece of Beef Wellington making sure to get pastry and the mushroom duxelle with it. He chewed and swallowed, taking pleasure in forcing his lackies to wait for his response. "I cannot wait any longer. I have already tasked Tanya with stepping up all the final collections. Report to her for reassignment."

He took another hefty slice of his Wellington, spearing a piece of poached asparagus, but this time his hand paused on its way to his mouth.

"Well?" Neither Wayne nor Boris had moved. "What are you waiting for? Go!"

Alone again just a few moments later, Earl Bacon grumpily pushed his plate to one side. His meal was going to ruin. No longer at the perfect temperature, he would have to wait for his chef to make a new one. He hated wasting food, especially good food. To the Earl there was no greater crime.

With a little tinkle of the bell he used to summon his wait staff, the Earl's table was cleared and reset.

"You wish for a fresh plate, Sir?" asked Chef Billy Gordon, a man of significant proportions hired because the Earl knew never to trust a skinny chef.

Automatically, Earl Bacon's mouth opened to confirm he wanted his entire meal over again, but did he? There was a niggling discomfort coming from within his centre. Not from his gut which he believed to be in superb health, but from somewhere in the centre of his chest. It was the strain of the last two days he decided once he'd sent his chef away and had time to quietly reflect.

Until two days ago Albert Smith could be considered a nuisance, a pain in the backside, but little more than that. It bothered the Earl that the old man had not only evaded capture in Cornwall but had then vanished without a trace. His operatives could not find him, but neither could the nation's police.

It beggared belief.

It also no longer mattered.

Three days ago Earl Hubert Bacon was contentedly taking his time. His larders were filling, his wine cellars too. Inside his vast underground complex there were crops being harvested and livestock producing a steady supply of eggs, milk, and meat. He had most of the people he needed, yet his list was far from complete.

The list wasn't exactly in the bin now, but significant portions of it were to be sacrificed for the sake of expediency. There just wasn't time to get it all. Not now.

Letting what he'd eaten settle – a key element to any robust meal in his educated and experienced opinion – he reached for the special edition of The Independent Enquirer. It was not a publication he read, but how could he avoid it when its subject was so sensational it was all the television news could talk about.

Filling the cover, an old picture of Albert Smith in his dress uniform looked out, his eyes boring into the Earl's as if in accusation.

The Independent Enquirer, a subdivision of a major national newspaper, specialised in big news articles where their investigative journalists could dig deep into the truth to deliver big headline-grabbing stories.

That's what this was and no mistake.

Albert Smith had become a news story in his own right and the Earl had revelled in past weeks as the police blamed the retired detective for the explosion in Whitstable and more besides. It seems they might do his job and rid the Earl of the annoyingly persistent old man. However, the special edition of The Independent Enquirer threw that all into doubt.

A journalist by the name Jessica Fletcher knew far more about Earl Bacon's operation than ought to be possible. It came first hand from Albert Smith, a man she met in Eton when he foiled a money laundering ring. In the article, the journalist and the team at The Independent Enquirer offered an alternative theory regarding Albert Smith: that he was a lone wolf investigator on the trail of a shadowy master criminal.

In truth, Earl Bacon rather liked being likened to a shadowy master criminal, but the fact they knew he existed was overwhelmingly disturbing, nevertheless.

The Independent Enquirer dug into a hidden spate of seemingly unrelated crimes from across Great Britain. They had eyewitness reports too and photographs showing the faces of three of his agents, Eugene, Francis, and Liam, who all died pursuing tasks at his behest. They travelled with fake identification, yet somehow their real names were displayed along with the part the journalists believed the men played.

Accounts from Arbroath, Keswick, Biggleswade and more along with the names of the people who worked with Albert to help foil the Earl's activities gave depth to the story. A lengthy section where Jessica interviewed Albert Smith's children and his neighbour, a decorated flying ace from the Royal Air Force, set straight the incidents in Reculver and Whitstable and provided credible reason why the old man was yet to come forward: he possessed no evidence with which he could convince the police.

There was even a section where The Independent Enquirer team speculated that similar crimes involving the disappearance of people and equipment from the food industry from places as far away as Japan could be part of the same spree.

Maddeningly, they were right in almost every case. Dozens of incidents were highlighted as part of a campaign being waged by a person they dubbed 'the Gastrothief'. The name, it seemed, was coined by Albert Smith when he needed a name for what he was seeing.

"The Gastrothief," Earl Bacon muttered to himself.

They knew all about him. Until two days ago when the story broke, Earl Bacon would happily have believed no one in the whole world had any idea he even existed. Except Albert Smith that is. Now everyone knew.

They didn't know where he was though, that was a saving grace. The lengthy report made it clear Albert Smith was on the hunt, but when Jessica Fletcher last spoke to him, he had no clue where the end of his search might lie.

Earl Hubert Bacon might have taken some small relief from this save for one rather worrying fact: Albert Smith had vanished. There was a rising social media campaign backing the old man and calling for the police to throw their resources into discovering the true identity of the shadowy master criminal 'the Gastrothief'.

Rubbing at his chest, he called for his physician, another man the Earl had chosen to 'save' from the impending doom the rest of the world's population faced. A pill, that would do it. Something to thin his blood perhaps.

Albert Smith had vanished which could be good news or bad. Yet since the police were still to locate him, the incompetent fools, Earl Bacon chose caution. He was shutting up shop. He had enough food – more than he could hope to eat in the years he had left. So what if there were a few delicacies he hadn't been able to obtain? In three days the doors to the outside world would close forever.

His underground bunker was impregnable. Once the doors were sealed there was no way in and no chance for those inside to get out. It meant that when the food finally did run out, the people inside would starve to death, but that would happen long after the Earl was dead and wasn't a factor that ever entered his mind.

The Earl rubbed at his chest again, unhappy that he wasn't going to get to kill Albert Smith. He abhorred violence, but considered that he might have made an exception for the old man.

Wondering why his physician was taking so long, he summoned Tanya. She had been his most loyal and capable agent, a ruthless woman who would kill without remorse and at the slightest provocation. When she returned from Cornwall having narrowly missed the opportunity to kill Albert Smith, she seemed ready to quit the Earl's employment and he'd been forced to convince her to stay.

Maybe Albert Smith was out there and maybe he wasn't; the Earl no longer cared. He could focus on revenge against the man who had cost him so much or he could beat him by denying Albert Smith the opportunity to win.

Tanya would oversee the final collections, pushing the other agents to make sure nothing was missed. She would get it done and then he would seal her and everyone else inside his underground bunker forever.

The Smell of Chips

R ex lifted his nose to the wind, sniffing deeply. Salty air from the sea filled his nostrils,
carrying with it a thousand scents Rex's canine nose filtered, labelled, and sorted.
He wasn't hungry, but the smell coming from a chip shop made his belly rumble all the
same.

The smell of grease-laden chips had the exact same effect on Albert. He was standing
next to Rex, watching the roads coming in and out of the town from a position near the
harbour. They were in a small Welsh village called Glan-Y-Wern where Albert hoped his
journey would end.

They arrived the previous evening, using darkness to cover their movements and limit the
number of people who might see them. It had taken five days to get to the remote fishing
village on the Atlantic coast from their start point in Cornwall; a deliberately slow journey
inspired by the need to get there, rather than get there quickly and risk not getting there
at all.

It could have been driven in perhaps three hours or a train would have achieved the same,
via a few changes, in five or six. Albert couldn't use public transport though, not if he
wanted to finish what he had started.

On the run from the police and certain the employees of the man he pursued would
approach him with an even less polite demeanour than the authorities, Albert knew he

was between a rock and a hard place. Innocent of all charges, blithely unaware of the article in The Independent Enquirer and the social media movement it sparked, and chasing a ghost the world in general denied could even exist, Albert believed his only chance was to catch the Gastrothief.

It was a stupid name for a master criminal, yet when Albert coined it, thoughts of anyone else ever saying the word never entered his mind.

A mid-sized goods vehicle broached the hill that led down toward the tiny Welsh village of Glan-Y-Wern. With little by way of leads to follow, Albert had chosen to use his eyes, a trick the younger generation rarely failed to consider. If they did, they would use a drone or some other unnecessary contraption.

The village boasted a population of just over a thousand residents, most of whom, Albert suspected, had been born there. It was that kind of place. The goods vehicle was a deep shade of green with gold livery along its sides. It was perhaps the tenth 'possible' in the last hour.

With one road leading into and then out of the village, Albert hoped he might spot a vehicle that was distinctly out of place. The Gastrothief, so called because he was stealing food, chefs, and ingredients, had a penchant for speciality dishes from across the nation. If a food truck bringing food produce from a distant part of the country came past, Albert knew it could only be heading to one place: the Gastrothief's lair.

Or his house, or wherever it was the man lived. Lair sounded more fitting as Albert knew of many kidnap victims taken by the master criminal's people. That they hadn't returned could only mean one of two things. They were either dead or, more palatably, were being held captive.

To do that meant armed guards or a facility from which they could not escape.

The green van came closer, piquing Albert's interest.

Rex turned to look when his human shifted position. He didn't care about staying in the same spot for hours at a time. He could while away his day dozing, and they had walked plenty in the last week. He was, however, getting hungry, the aroma from the chippy doing him no favours whatsoever.

Albert made a silent bet with himself – this was going to be it. The green van would have to pass right by him unless it turned off and into one of the village backstreets. The goods vehicle could be carrying fresh Cromer crab from the beaches of Norfolk, Panackelty from Sunderland, or Groaty Pudding from the Black Country. If it were any of those things or something similar there could be no reason for it to be here unless it had been hijacked/stolen by agents of the Gastrothief.

Help was just a phone call away. So too was arrest and incarceration. If he could find the Gastrothief's hiding place. If he could prove there were prisoners being held against their will and a stockpile of stolen goods from across the country, then he could contact his children. All three were senior police detectives with the ability to organise an armed raid.

He would still get arrested and answer questions, but the truth behind his unheeded claims would be undeniable. It wasn't about victory or glory; Albert's only desire was to be allowed to return home.

The green van vanished from sight as the road descended through green fields and into the village. Forty seconds later, it swung into view again on the harbour road. Coming straight for Albert now, he couldn't read what was written on the side, but he soon would.

Obviously, if it was what he hoped for, the vehicle would be gone and out of sight within seconds. He couldn't chase after it, but he would have a direction, and a lone taxi outside the tiny train station would be able to take him for a ride. Maybe he would find it, maybe he wouldn't, but it was all he had.

Well, not quite. He had one other clue to follow. The same clue that led him to the Welsh coast.

Holding his breath with anticipation when the goods vehicle came by, Albert's eyes flicked over the words printed on its flank.

'Preston's Premier Plumbing Services'.

Disappointment left his nose in a huff, and he closed his eyes for a moment to gather his thoughts. There was no point allowing his emotions to tip the balance in the Gastrothief's favour. Rushing to find that which he sought would only result in a premature end to his quest. Patience was his ally.

Flicking his eyelids open, Albert squared his jaw and with a click of his tongue he set off down the street.

"Some chips for lunch, Rex?" he asked, looking down to meet his dog's eyes when Rex looked up.

Giving an excited wag of his tail, for he knew when he was being invited to eat, Rex increased his pace.

As an indicator to show how quiet the village truly was, the chip shop was only open three days a week, from lunch on Friday to lunch on Sunday. At a little after noon on a Saturday, Albert expected there to be a small queue.

"Are you always this quiet?" he asked upon approaching the empty counter.

Behind it, a woman in her forties and an Indian man who Albert took to be the proprietor, looked up.

The Indian man offered a shopkeeper's smile. "You're a little ahead of the lunchtime rush."

They had been open for an hour, presumably to get the oil up to temperature and prepare whatever they were going to fry. They were yet to cook anything though because the glass cabinet to display fish, pies, and other offerings was devoid of life.

"What can I get you?" asked the woman.

To her rear, an old-fashioned board, the kind one pushed small, coloured plastic letters and numbers into holes, showed the menu. It was as full of choices as one might find anywhere else across the nation.

"Just a small portion of chips, I think," Albert squinted at the menu. Tempted by the cod and the plaice, he knew eating much more than a few chips now would mean he had no appetite later.

Rex nudged his leg, a single eyebrow raised when Albert looked down.

"Ah, yes, perhaps that should be a medium sized portion."

"It's small or large," the woman replied, her tone not exactly surly or bored, but a long way from engaging.

The Indian gentleman stepped in to say, "We have a pensioner's portion, Pamela."

Pamela elected to offer no comment, moments later depositing ready-cut pieces of potato into an industrial sized fryer.

Albert retreated to a corner where three plastic chairs lined one wall. His face had been on the television – something that tends to happen when the police suspect you of terrorism – yet he wasn't too worried about being identified.

Though he travelled with a large German Shepherd dog, the one thing that ought to make him easy to spot, the picture his children supplied was an old one and he'd done what he could to alter his appearance. Not in an overt way with a false nose and a set of plastic glasses complete with comedy eyebrows, but by dressing differently and by letting his facial hair grow.

It had been a week since he last shaved, a period longer than he could remember ever going without removing his whiskers. Well, there was the moustache he wore for almost a year in the seventies before Petunia, his wife, asked him to remove it.

The white stubble altered the shape of his face, but a parka coat, which he found in a charity shop hid most of his face from sight. He'd not seen a parka coat in years. His eldest son, Gary, had worn one to school when they were the fashion. Zipping right up around the face with a fur trim, it was nigh impossible to see the person inside with any degree of clarity.

Topping it off, Albert had found a pair of glasses in the same shop as the coat. They had a thick rim and covered a lot of his face. They gave him a headache if he wore them for too long, but were a low prescription strength and he could see with them on. His disguise extended beyond the coat, beard, and glasses, but that was for when he had to take the coat off.

A woman walked into the shop with a child holding her hand. The youngster was three or four, clinging to his mother who looked flustered and tired.

She glanced Albert's way, but only to check he wasn't waiting to order.

Turning to look out the glass front of the chip shop, Albert thought about his next step.

A single clue brought him to Wales: the stub from a betting slip. The address on it was a street in Glan-Y-Wern and he knew the name of the man who placed the bet. His first name at least. Liam died in Cornwall, cut down with a blast from a shotgun, so would not be returning to the turf accountant.

It placed one of the Gastrothief's agents in Glan-Y-Wern, leaving Albert with the fervent hope it was not a red herring.

Had Liam's accent been Welsh, Albert might have assumed this was his hometown. He wasn't Welsh though. Not even close. Albert only heard him speak a few words but that was enough to know he hailed from the northeast of England.

So he had a man connected with the Gastrothief who was familiar enough with a small village in Wales to be placing bets there.

Albert would have been there first thing this morning, but the turf accountant kept much the same hours as the chip shop. It opened at noon, but Albert had watched the premises from his position on the harbour and the queue of men outside dictated he ought to wait before wandering in to ask questions.

With chips in hand and Rex's nose inches from the bag, Albert returned to his vigil against the harbour wall. Behind him a small fleet of fishing boats were returning or had already moored to offload their catch.

Betting Shop Blues

Rex never gave a lot of thought to what might be next. Like all dogs, he lived in the moment, never thinking of the past unless it had a connection to his present. They were somewhere new, and he was with his human – what more could he ask for? Well, food, obviously, and he had that too. The old man never made him go hungry, there was always something on offer.

The squawk of a seagull high above pulled Rex's eyes skyward. It peered down at him, joined by another that whipped from left to right for a better view.

Would they attempt to steal the chips?

Rex swallowed the hot, greasy delights but didn't duck his head to pick up more from the pile his human was good enough to place on the ground. Instead, he took a moment to threaten the seagull.

They were an old enemy, but beating them in the past gave him confidence. Top lip curled back to expose his teeth, Rex grumbled darkly.

Lost in his own thoughts, Albert twitched to see what had his dog on edge. Tracking his eyes upward, he laughed and reached out with greasy fingers to ruffle the fur on Rex's neck.

"Pay them no mind, Rex."

The seagulls squawked again, wheeling high above held aloft by the breeze. Rex watched, unable to enjoy his lunch when he knew what seagulls were capable of in sufficient numbers. Only when his human pushed a chip from his share of the bag under Rex's nose, did he return to the task of eating.

Chips eaten and bellies full, Albert knew that to put off visiting the betting shop any longer would be cowardice on his part. Ordinarily, he would have no reason to resist marching into the business to quiz the people inside about the man he met in Cornwall: Did he come in alone or were there friends they could describe? How long had he been placing bets with them? Did they know anything more about him? His name? Did he drive a car? Was there CCTV footage?

It was so much easier to consider such tasks when one's likeness isn't being broadcast on the news.

Acknowledging that he either needed to get on with it or give up and hand himself over to the police, Albert levered himself off the bench on which he sat. With feet aimed across the road, he made a beeline for the betting shop.

Rex trotted happily at his human's side. He didn't know where they were going and didn't much care. They were out. They were together. It was fun.

The betting shop wasn't empty as Albert hoped it might be - attracting the attention of a member of staff so he could get a conversation going and carefully drop in a few clever questions was hard enough without other people listening. What if one or more of the men placing bets worked for the Gastrothief? Liam visited the premises, why wouldn't anyone else?

If anything, Albert was hoping that would be the case. Anyone with an accent that wasn't local would be worth following. They might lead him directly to the Gastrothief and the whole ordeal could be over.

Thankfully, he didn't have to feel like he was out of place or worry that he might fumble his words; he had a ruse already in mind.

In his seventy-eight years on the planet, Albert Smith had placed the sum total of one bet. It was a couple of months ago in Melton Mowbray when once again he was trying to obtain information and ended up placing a bet just to keep the proprietor talking.

He had the betting slip from that transaction in his wallet ready to produce today because, by a blind stroke of serendipity, the shop he was now entering was from the same chain. Could they check if the horse he'd bet on had won? Albert didn't know, but was about to find out.

Rex padded over the threshold when his human held the door for him. The air inside contained the scent of men. Only men. Rex could tell women had been inside, but not today. One of the men was suffering some gastric distress, quietly venting gas to the atmosphere while imagining no one else could smell it.

Albert paused inside the door, not wanting to look like he was on unfamiliar ground but unable to avoid the obvious need to orientate himself.

The same betting machines he recognised and vaguely remembered from Melton Mowbray were arranged in banks of three along the walls and in the middle of the shop. Opposite the entrance, a counter with two men positioned to take money from hopeful punters, and prowling the floor to give advice where opportunity arose to extract more of their hard-earned money, the manager.

Good. The manager would do.

First, he needed to remove the hood of his coat. It was one thing to hide inside its recesses outside, or for brief interactions. Another entirely to attempt a conversation when it would look like he was trying to hide his face. Plus, Albert was certain the hood muffled his voice and certainly played tricks on his hearing.

Standing just inside the door, Albert reached up with both hands to reveal the second part of his disguise. Again, it was a chance find that provided the dog collar and black shirt that made him look quite distinctively like a member of the clergy.

As disguises went, Albert believed it was a little weak for it did nothing to alter or hide his features, yet hoped people would remember the vicar and not the man.

"Hello," Albert approached the potbellied man wearing a waistcoat in the betting shop's livery. "I need a little help if you are available." Albert accepted that getting what he wanted today might cost him some money in the form of placing another bet, but it was a small price to pay. In fact, the only factor that caused irritation was his inability to spend his own money.

Bankrolled by a friend so the police couldn't track his location through Albert's own bank transactions, that he might spend that same friend's money on something so frivolous as gambling was extremely irksome.

The manager, Curtis Jones, stood six feet and three inches tall, was skinny as a bean pole – his nickname through school – and was going bald fast. Spending more time exercising his right arm as it lifted pint glasses in the Old Seamaster, his belly had swollen like that of a woman in the later stages of pregnancy. His wife did not approve.

Curtis Jones fixed Albert with a helpful grin – nothing would please him more than to help the old man extract the money from his wallet to then deposit it in the firm's bulging account - there were bonuses to be earned. He had a wife who wasn't necessarily demanding, but made it clear she wanted more than they had. That required more money.

"Of course. That's what I'm here for."

The other clientele in the shop glanced his way but none bothered to look for long – it was just an old vicar with a dog.

Albert took out his wallet, noting the manager's eyes flaring when he saw it.

"I have ... I placed a bet a short while ago. It wasn't here," he clarified, "I was in Melton Mowbray at the time. This betting malarky is all a bit new to me and I've never figured out how to check whether I won or lost. It was fun though ... that thrill of the chase, I guess. So I want to see how my horse did, and then maybe seek some advice about how to go about investing some more of my pension in the chance of winning big." Albert made sure to sound excited at the concept; he wanted the man to believe he was going to hook Albert for a big sale.

The manager's professional smile never left his face. However, his eyes betrayed the questions roiling inside.

"Are members of the clergy permitted to gamble?" he asked the question even though the vicar to his front clearly intended to do just that.

In all honesty, Albert didn't know the answer to the question, but had a response lined up anyway.

With a snort of laughter, he said, "Provided we don't gamble the donations." Looking around to share his amusement with the shop's other patrons, Albert succeeded in making them return to what they were doing.

"Now, I'm sure a stout fellow like you can help a chap out," Albert steered the manager away from the door. "Here's the receipt for that bet I made in Melton Mowbray." Albert handed over the now creased and tired slip of paper the machine had given in exchange for his thirty pounds. Slowly, that was how to do this - talk about the old bet, the new bet and money, then swing carefully to the subject of Liam and whether he was known.

It was accepted with a smile, the manager's focus swinging down to look at his hands where a moment or two later his smile froze.

Albert had to watch the man's eyes flicker across it more than once. There was something wrong, and though Albert had no reason to believe there was anything on the receipt to say who he was, a worrying ball of dread materialised at his core.

Did the slip of paper have his name on it? He could swear it didn't. Squinting to see now, the man wasn't holding it still enough for Albert to make out the printed words.

"You say you placed this bet in Melton Mowbray?" the manager sought to confirm.

Trying to avoid sounding guilty, Albert said, "Yes, why?"

Rex looked up at his human. His scent had changed. Something was bothering him.

Albert felt Rex nudge his leg, the dog's wet nose leaving a small damp spot on his trousers no doubt, but he couldn't break eye contact with the man holding his betting slip. What should he do? Wait until the manager's back was turned and leave the shop? If he snuck away perhaps the fellow would let it go, uncertain that he was, in fact, talking to a man the police wanted.

Albert's heart pounded.

"Sorry," the manager stammered, his face seemingly unable to decide which emotion to display. He looked nervous and excited at the same time. "I just need to check something. Could you wait here for just a moment, please? I'll be right back."

He didn't wait for Albert's response, choosing to spin on his heels and head toward a door at the back of the shop before he'd finished speaking. One of the men behind the counter found himself speared by the manager's gaze, an unspoken but obviously urgent message passing between them.

When the man behind the counter twitched his eyes in Albert's direction, his expression was impossible to read, yet Albert took the wide eyes of surprise to be a bad sign.

The moment the manager swiped a card to access the rear of the shop and the staffs' attention was no longer on him, Albert reversed until his backside hit the door and then kept going.

Outside in the street he was just as visible through the floor to ceiling glass windows. With no time to lose, he turned right and got out of sight. A glance told him they hadn't seen him leave, but it wasn't going to take them long to notice.

The police would come. It would be slow in this part of the world unless the village had a local bobby. That was possible, but Albert doubted it; that kind of community policing had stopped some time ago.

At the first opportunity, Albert made a turn. It was into an alley between two houses but looked to go all the way through to the next street. Anything to throw them off his scent so they couldn't tell the police which way he might have gone.

Only once he was a couple of streets away did he breathe a sigh of relief.

Was it relief though? What did he do now? Was he even in the right place?

Self-Pity

Wanting to get off the streets and telling himself he needed to gather his thoughts, Albert returned to his bed and breakfast.

Thistle-Do-Me, a pleasant render-fronted detached bungalow at the end of a street and on a rise overlooking the harbour, had four guest rooms, and was run by a married couple. Albert thought of them as young though they were in their forties. Their two children were at boarding school, a throwback from the husband's recently-ended military career.

They were the kind of people you knew everything about five minutes after meeting them because they got it all off their chest like it was a confession.

No longer able to use Roy Hope's credit card for certain knowledge the police would be watching, he'd paid for the room with cash. That would not have worked at a hotel or any larger establishment, but off season in the middle of nowhere, the B&B's owners didn't even blink.

The disguise had worked in his favour, of course – who could be more trustworthy than a vicar? Selling them on the idea that he was a retired member of the clergy seeking solace and solitude as he communed with God in his final years, they gave what they promised was their best room and let him be.

Back in it now, he wondered if the bedside table might contain a bible. He felt like he could use the help.

"What do you think, Rex?" he asked, ruffling and scratching the thick fur on his dog's neck. "Have we hit a dead end?"

Rex had his head on the old man's knees, his eyes closed to revel in the closeness they shared. When Albert spoke, Rex opened his eyes to look up. He knew he'd been asked a question; the cadence of the words gave it away, but he didn't understand what it meant. Rex liked to think he was pretty good at understanding humans – their language wasn't that complicated, and they used the same words over and over which made them easy to learn.

There were subtleties though, and humans would throw in new words to confuse him. In recent weeks, Rex knew there was a crime to solve because he either saw it take place or the clues were obvious. Words like 'murder' or 'robbery' were easy to understand. They set him on the right path, allowing Rex to employ his vastly superior canine senses to find the guilty person behind each crime.

The old man helped where he could, examining clues or reading things – a skill Rex didn't exactly understand, but today there was no crime to solve. Unable to rationalise his life in terms of days, weeks, and months, Rex nevertheless knew they had been moving about from place to place for a long time. The trees had been full of leaves when they set off, his human dressed in just a shirt and jacket.

It was cooler now, turning to cold and the leaves had long since accepted the ravages of the changing seasons.

Everywhere they went they encountered another mystery to unravel. Except this time. Was that what had his human feeling sad? Imparting warmth and love, Rex nuzzled at the old man's hands and wondered what he could do to help lift his mood.

Albert had enough years behind him to be able to recognise he was at low ebb. The sense of defeat pummelling his emotions would pass, but looking out the window at the boats bobbing on the light chop in the harbour, he wanted to crawl into bed and sleep until it was all over.

It wasn't the first time in his life things hadn't gone his way. In his career as a police detective, it was often when he felt least able to solve a case that a small, and previously insignificant clue would suddenly reignite the investigation.

Unfortunately, as he tried hard to force himself to rally and refused to give into pity, Albert knew in his heart he had reached the end of the road. He'd given it a good shot; he could say that, and no one could ever take it away from him.

However, failure on his part didn't just mean arrest, interrogation, and embarrassment for his family. It meant he was failing to rescue those persons he knew to be held captive by the Gastrothief.

His eyes stopped moving. His whole face froze solid, and his next breath found itself forced to wait until he was ready.

Rex sensed the change instantly, lifting his head and rising quickly to his feet.

Albert could scarcely believe what he was looking at. How had he not seen it before? How could he have been so dumb to have not looked for it?

Rex barked, concerned his human was having a seizure.

Albert jerked up and out of his chair by the window. No longer feeling sorry for himself, he said, "Come along, Rex. The game is afoot!"

A Hint of a Clue

"Going out again, Vicar?" asked Malory Hunt, the landlady, when Albert rushed by at the foot of the stairs.

He was hurriedly stuffing both arms into his coat and had his wallet clamped between his teeth. Unable to reply until he could get a hand free, his jacket sleeves did their best to fight and defeat him.

"I was about to ask if you wanted some tea?" Malory added.

A final thrust with both arms shot his hands through the cuffs and he spat out his wallet to catch it in his right hand.

"Sorry," Albert chuckled, reminding himself that a man of God would be evenly tempered at all times. "Rex needs another walk."

"No, I don't," Rex frowned. "I mean, I'm happy to go out. Unless, you know, there's food to be had. I believe the lady said something about tea?" Rex's nose was trying to detect the presence of biscuits.

Aware that he was lying while wearing a dog collar, Albert forged ahead. "Thank you for the offer of tea. I'll take a rain check if I may." With a pace toward the door, Albert reconsidered. "Ah, I might have a few questions when I get back if that's okay?"

The landlady's forehead creased slightly. "Questions?"

"About the local area," Albert clarified. "For instance, are there any big houses around here?"

"Big houses?" Malory repeated his words again.

Rex wanted to know if they were going out or not. He hadn't needed to pee until his human raised the subject. Now it was all he could think of. Well, that and the possibility of biscuits.

How to pose questions about the Gastrothief was something Albert had been struggling to figure out since before he arrived in Glan-Y-Wern. With only a vague idea what he was looking for and no wish to raise suspicions, he wasn't even sure what to ask.

"Yes. Like a manor house or a facility that might house lots of people ..." Albert voiced trailed off. He wasn't making sense and what was he really asking? The Gastrothief was here, he was certain of that now, but he could be set up in a factory for all Albert knew. He believed there must be armed guards to keep the prisoners inside, but how would it look if he started asking questions about gunmen?

His landlady was already eyeing Albert with a mix of curiosity and suspicion (at least in Albert's head, she was).

"No, Vicar, there's nothing like that in Glan-Y-Wern."

Albert backed to the door to let Rex out. "No, of course. I was just curious." He thought of a lie to cover his interest. "I'm a fan of stately homes and such. I just love looking around the architecture."

"Oh," Malory remarked. "Well, the only place like that for miles is the old earl's place."

Albert had the door open a crack and almost caught Rex's nose when he shut it again.

"Earl's place?"

Malory nodded. "Yes. It's about two miles away, though there's nothing between here and there. Joshua and I have not been living here long as you know, but I believe the entire village used to be part of the estate. It was sold a few years ago, apparently. Some Arab family bought it. There was quite a bit of controversy. I couldn't tell you what happened to the earl though."

"He moved away?"

Malory shrugged. "I don't think he died. He had no family though; I do remember hearing that much. People like to gossip, you know. Oh," Malory looked as though something had just occurred to her, "I need to let you know that Joshua and I will not be here this evening."

Albert tipped an eyebrow; she clearly had more she wanted to say.

"It's our anniversary."

"Oh, wonderful," Albert fell into the role of vicar again. "Blessings upon you."

"Yes, thank you. Well, anyway Joshua has arranged something special, apparently and we will be out until late. You have a key, yes?"

Albert reached into a pocket to produce the single Yale key on a leather fob.

"Jolly good. You can let yourself in and make yourself at home. We'll be here to do breakfast in the morning."

Albert thanked his landlady and set off toward the harbour once more.

There was no sign that the manager at the bookkeepers had called the police. Albert had watched for it and listened too. From his room at the bed and breakfast, he could see the main road sweeping through the village. No police had come. Perhaps they wouldn't, he mused. Perhaps he'd overreacted when the manager took his betting slip.

So what had affected the man so?

26

Bet Your Life

"What do you mean he left the shop? Why would he have left the shop?" Robert Grand, president of Grand Turf Accountant didn't understand what he was being told.

"Just what I said, Mr Grand," replied Curtis Jones, manager of the outlet in Glan-Y-Wern. "I turned my back, and he was gone. No one saw him go either." He held the crumpled betting slip in his hand like it was a winning lottery ticket which, essentially, it was.

The story was a bizarre one to say the least and one that Robert had been against promoting from the very start. According to Colin Masters, the manager of the outlet in Melton Mowbray, an old man wandered in one day with a teenage girl and a German Shepherd dog in tow.

He acted as if he had no idea what he was doing, yet managed to not only pick out the longest shot running in any race that day, but in doing so discovered an overlooked nag with legs like greased lightning. With Colin Masters' help, the old man placed an accumulator bet that would continue running until the person holding the ticket chose to cash it in.

Normally, Robert Grand would approve such a bet with raucous delight. The chances of winning were next to zero, so even though it was a small wager, it represented how the average man in the street could be encouraged to hand over their money. Surely, it was better in his pocket than anyone else's?

The stupid horse kept winning though.

The odds on the horse shortened, obviously, but that was for an individual race, not an accumulator. With an accumulator, the odds of continuing to win got longer and longer. Sooner or later, almost everyone who ever took out that kind of bet, stayed in it too long and lost the lot.

In many ways it was one of the safest bets for the bookie, yet somehow an old man from Melton Mowbray was holding his nerve. There had to be ice-water in his veins. According to the manager in Melton Mowbray, the old man had never even been back in to check what his winnings had amounted to thus far.

Did he really not understand how much money he had won? The speculation about the firm was that he had to be someone from the industry. Colin Masters had been played. But when they checked the name – it was recorded on the transaction when he paid – there was no trace of him working for anyone else. He wasn't even at the horse end of things.

That was weeks ago, and Robert had given it little thought since – he was too busy to worry about a problem that might never come. The man would lose it eventually and that would be that.

Until today. Until now. Now there was a man with the betting slip in a small village in Wales of all places. The remoteness of his appearance suggested something untoward or underhand - certainly enough to get Robert Grand's senses twitching. Far more damning was the news that the old man fled the shop mere moments after handing over the ticket.

"Have you ever seen him before?" Robert repeated a question the man at the other end had already answered. "You're sure this was his first time in the shop?"

Curtis Jones needed no time to consider his answer. "Yes, Mr Grand. He's definitely not a regular and his accent was English. London area would be my guess. What should we do, Sir? If he's staying in the village, it shouldn't take long to figure out where he is. There can't be many visiting priests."

Robert Grand blurted, "What was that? Did you just say priest?" He'd been trying to figure out whether this was a PR opportunity or an impending disaster. One thing was for sure, he wasn't going to manage it. If the press got hold of the story and it went against them, the backlash could topple their stock. He was a major shareholder, but not the only one and there had already been calls to replace him from more than one.

"Yes, Mr Grand. The man in question is a vicar. Should I find out where he is staying?"

Curtis imagined the publicity his little shop would get if he could be the one to hail the winner. The priest said he wanted to see if he had won. He made it sound like he had no idea. A thirty pound bet turned into a small fortune? It was almost unheard of and would bring in the punters to place their bets faster than any advertising campaign. Surely Mr Grand could see that?

Robert Grand sucked on his lip for a second. Who could he delegate this to? He loved delegating. If they got it wrong, it was their incompetence because they failed to follow his instructions. If they got it right, well that was a mark of his excellent leadership.

First, he needed to check something. He'd just looked up the customer's name: Albert Smith. There was something familiar about it. Something in the deep recesses of Robert's brain insisting the name was somehow important.

To end the call, he said, "Do nothing. Is that understood? I will have a PR executive contact you shortly."

"Will we get to announce the winner here ..." Curtis stopped talking because the line had gone dead. The head of the firm had hung up.

Someone from PR would be in touch. Well, he would toe the line and do nothing, but that didn't mean he couldn't find out where the vicar was staying. If he was in town, someone would know about it.

Harbour Answers

S tanding at the harbour wall, Albert stared down at the boats. Or rather, he stared at one in particular. Was it really there earlier and he just didn't see it? Okay, so he hadn't been looking for it, but there was no mistaking the sleek sunseeker style yacht. It stood out against the other vessels in the dockyard, most of which were working boats kitted out to catch fish or shellfish of some kind. They were rough, ready, and in stark contrast to the glistening blue and white hulled millionaire's toy at the far end of one jetty.

Was it the same boat?

Determining that was where things got dicey. If there was someone on board, they would see him approaching long before he saw them. Worse yet, if they had moored to go into the village for something, they might be about to return. He could easily get trapped.

There really was no good scenario, so Albert grumbled a few curse words under his breath and walked down to the pontoons.

Rex mostly watched the sky. There were seagulls above him again, drifting on the wind as they watched the ground below. What he needed, Rex observed, was a distraction. Food of almost any kind would do it.

One of the fishermen threw a bucket of fish guts overboard. The splosh came a heartbeat later when they hit the sea, but by then a dozen or more of the big white birds were swooping to claim the prize.

It wasn't in Rex's nature to give up food, but if there was ever a need to send the birds one way when he went the other, that was how he would want to do it.

The ground moved beneath his feet giving him cause to stop walking.

Albert gave his lead a gentle tug. "Come on, Rex. I think we ought to be quick about this. Just in case."

They were on the pontoons, floating wooden boards arranged laterally. They shifted again with the next wave. Through a gap between his feet, Rex could see the inky, cold water. It reminded him of Cornwall and the dip he took there.

Planting his backside rather than going any further, it was then that his eyes caught sight of a familiar shape. Not wanting to trust them, Rex sniffed deeply, and guided by his curiosity, he started walking again.

"That's it, Rex. Good boy. We don't need to be here long. I just want to be certain that's the right boat."

A scent Rex had lodged in his head arrived on the breeze. Instantly his hackles raised, and his top lip curled away from his teeth.

Tanya.

He knew her name from hearing his human say it. She had hit him with a stun gun (not that Rex knew what that was) at a house in Kent and threw him overboard to drown at sea in Cornwall. She almost blew him to smithereens on a beach in Whitstable and it was way past time to even the score. It wasn't revenge he wanted, it was protection for his human. Tanya was bad news and though her scent was barely there, Rex knew she had been on the boat recently.

Albert heard Rex's growling, but if he hadn't, the dog's sudden change in attitude would have caught his attention. Rex leapt forward, straining against Albert's grip as he sought to attack.

Rex wanted to get to the boat. He could get on board easily enough at the back end where it was moored. Anyone he found who didn't smell right was going to get bitten.

"Whoa, boy. Slow down." Albert reeled Rex in. Coming down to his level, and placing a knee on the damp wood of the pontoon, Albert put a soothing arm around Rex's shoulders. "You can tell, can't you?" he nodded to himself. "I sometimes wonder if you might just be the best detective I've ever worked with."

Rex licked Albert's nose: he'd been thinking the exact same thing. The wily old man had found the bad people again. Rex marvelled at how his human could travel so far yet fetch up where Tanya's scent lingered.

She would not be alone, Rex felt certain; she never had been before. Leaning into an onshore breeze, he sucked in a noseful of air. Filtering out the fish, salt, pollution, and a million other smells, he sought the scent of any humans he recognised.

Albert used a hand to push off the ground. His knees were not what they used to be. Heck, none of him was what it used to be, so a shove to get himself moving helped when he needed to get back to his feet.

Upright again, and convinced he was once again in the right place, he threw caution to the wind and walked right up to the boat.

If there was someone on board, he would give them a face full of Rex. It looked empty though. Staring in through a closed door, he could see the interior. No lights were on to indicate someone might be below deck and when he looked more closely, he saw a padlock securing the door in place.

That someone might be captive below deck swum into his head and got flushed out again. He thought it not only unlikely, but too dangerous for him to investigate.

He noted the name printed in big, blue letters across the stern 'Second Helpings' but since he hadn't seen the boat's name when he came across it in Cornwall, it meant nothing.

Or did it?

With nothing to gain by hanging around in such an exposed position, Albert wasted no time in returning to land. Stepping off the last piece of pontoon, he looked around to find anything that looked like an office.

There was nothing. Well, nothing except a small shack, the kind a chap put in the garden to keep the fork, spade, and lawnmower in. It looked serviceable and had a window on one side to let in daylight. Someone was in there; Albert saw them move.

Setting off, he tapped Rex on his shoulder.

"Be on the lookout, Rex. I'm sure the name 'Tanya' means nothing to you, but if you can remember the woman who shot you in the backside with a taser, then keep an eye or a nose out for her."

Rex didn't need to be told. His senses were already attuned to detect any person he knew from their travels. Also, the scent of another dog was around. The smell was unavoidable, Rex noting it when they first arrived at the harbour this morning. It was everywhere, which to Rex meant the dog was resident. No one could mark so many surfaces without being in the area full time.

The door of the little shack swung open before Albert could reach it. The hood of his parka hid his face, but accepting it was no way to gain trust if he was to ask questions, he took it down and made sure to expose his dog collar.

It caught the person coming out to meet him by surprise.

"Oh, I was just about to say something rude," said the woman. "I'm rather glad I didn't now."

"Hello," Albert extended his right hand. "Reverend Roy Hope." he gave the name of his neighbour in Kent. "Sorry, was I trespassing?"

"No, not exactly," the woman thought carefully about what she wanted to say. "I thought you were going to try to get on the yacht. I'm rather glad you didn't. That sort of thing doesn't go down very well around here. Shelley Rankin, by the way."

Shelley was in her mid-fifties, short and stout with an ample bosom hidden beneath a thick woollen jumper. A woollen hat covered her head, wisps of curly, dark brown hair sticking out at the front, sides, and back. Her complexion could only be described as ruddy; that reddish hue one gets from excessive drinking or continual exposure to harsh elements.

"Oh, I was just admiring it," Albert remarked, lying through his teeth but doing so consciously as he steered ever so gently toward a question. "One of my parishioners used to have one just like it. He won the lottery, you know. He and his wife, I suppose." With a laugh he added, "I always wondered what percentage of my congregation prayed for the same each week. It's not theirs though; the name is different."

Shelley listened, not wanting to encourage the old priest to take up any more of her day – she had a crossword she was working on – but also unable to dismiss a vicar as she would anyone else.

"You said going any closer would not be well received," Albert reminded her. "Why is that?"

Expecting the dog he could smell to be inside the shack, Rex was not disappointed. An old beagle looked up from a saggy, dirty bed in the corner when he caught a whiff of the German Shepherd. Contentedly dreaming about finding an untended butcher's shop until a few moments ago, he looked at Rex with a sideways expression. The jowls on the left of his face were stuck to his gums, distorting the symmetry of his head. He gave it a shake and stood up.

"You're new," the beagle observed. "Just passing through?"

Rex wagged his tail. "Probably. I never can tell with my human. We move around a lot. You're here all the time, right?"

34

The beagle stretched, pushing his front paws out to flatten his chest to the floor and then arch his back and stretch off his back legs one at a time, he was in no hurry to give an answer.

When he was ready, he said, "Been here my whole life. Never really left, truth be told. I'm Harold, the harbour dog."

"The boat ..." Rex started.

Harold stopped him. "Got a lot of boats here, pup. You'll need to be more specific."

Rex thought for a second. "The one that doesn't smell of fish."

"Gotcha. The power-yacht. Fancy thing. Not sure what good it is if you can't catch fish though. Go on. What about it?"

While Rex quizzed the harbour dog about the people he saw coming and going from it, Albert was doing pretty much the same thing with Shelley.

"So you have a record of who it belongs to?" he enquired. Teasing information from her, he now knew the yacht docked four days ago – about right given it left Cornwall roughly six days ago. Albert wanted to show her a picture of Kelley, the woman he knew to have escaped on the boat with Tanya after the shootout with Cody on the quayside in Looe. He couldn't think how to do that though, not without generating a lot of questions he would not want to answer.

Instead, he asked about the yacht's ownership.

Shelley eyed him with suspicion. "That's not the sort of information I am at liberty to give out," she replied. In her head, she was questioning who the old priest might be. There was something about him that troubled her.

Albert said, "Of course. Good for you. Nice to find a person with integrity." Had he thought a bribe might work, he would be reaching for his wallet. Instead, he suspected such a move would drive the harbour lady to question his claim to be a man of the cloth.

"Why would you want to know that anyway, vicar?"

Now he was stuck. Scrambling to give a believable response, he said, "I was just curious. It seems so out of place and fancy for its surroundings." The words were out of his mouth before he could think them through and hear how insulting they might sound. Quickly, he added, "I wondered if the yacht might belong to someone famous. My, ah, granddaughter," he thought of Apple-Blossom, "is a big follower of the 'newly-famous'." He made air quotes. "She would love to have a snap of the latest reality TV star."

"Oh," Shelley bought Albert's lie. "Well, it's nothing like that I'm afraid. It belongs to an earl."

Albert breathed a sigh of relief. However, as he congratulated himself for thinking on his feet, his brain caught up with what Shelley had just said.

"An earl? Would that be the chap who used to live in a big house not so very far from here?"

Shelley's right eyebrow twitched. "That's right. You're rather well informed. Didn't you say you arrived yesterday?"

"Oh, I was chatting with my landlady earlier. She told me about him in a general history of the area kind of way. Said he up and sold his stately home and then vanished."

"Might have done. I heard something about it, but if it's not to do with fish, weather, or the harbour, I don't pay much attention," she laughed heartily, clearly believing she had said something funny.

"Do you ever see the earl then?" Albert leaned in to hear the answer. Was he about to make a giant discovery?

Below them, Rex was getting everything he could from Harold the harbour dog and unlike his human, needed to employ no subterfuge.

"Yeah, I think that's about right," Harold checked his memory. "Two female humans, breeding age but not in season when they came past me."

Unable to describe a smell, Rex had been forced to rely on his ability to outline Tanya's distinctive features. Not tall for a female, not a child but not old. Black hair and athletic which stood her apart from most other humans. If she was with another female human, the second woman's features would be much the same. Rex saw Kelly in Cornwall, but with no reason to do so until later, he had paid little attention to her physical shape.

"When were they last here?" Rex pressed Harold.

Harold scratched at his right ear with a back leg in an absentminded manner while he gave the question some thought.

"Not today," he concluded. Most dogs perceive time in terms of now. The sun came up and went down again some time later. The bit in between was divided into before breakfast, after breakfast, before dinner, after dinner, treat time, bedtime biscuit, et cetera. Rex had a better grasp on the passage of time than most, but he wasn't going to get a good steer from Harold.

Rex accepted the harbour dog's response. Tanya's scent lingered near the boat which had to mean she touched it recently. If not today, then it would be the last time the sun was up. Or at night, in the period in between days.

It placed her in his vicinity. She was guilty of crimes and Rex's sense of justice, hammered into him at the police dog academy, demanded he pursue her if he could. What he needed now was a direction to follow.

Above the dogs, Albert wasn't sure how he should feel. On the face of it, the earl sounded like a great candidate to be the Gastrothief. The man mysteriously vanished after selling his stately home. That wasn't exactly a whole lot to go on, but it was a whole lot more than he had before. If Shelley had her facts straight, the earl was the owner of a yacht Albert last saw being piloted by Tanya, one of the Gastrothief's agents.

Shelley knew nothing more than who owned the yacht and wasn't willing to look up the earl's full name or current address, not even for a vicar. Sensing she was becoming defensive with her answers and probably felt that she'd already revealed too much, Albert decided to quit while he was still ahead.

With a generous thank you and a blessing because he had no idea how a retired vicar ought to act and felt awkward doing nothing, Albert bade Shelley a good day and tried to leave.

"What did you say your name was again, vicar?" Shelley asked, stepping out of her shack for the first time. The suspicious tremor in her voice was unmistakable.

Albert silently acknowledged that if he were the bad guy in his tale, this would be where he chose to kill his next victim. She knew there was something amiss and was probing to satisfy her curiosity. Did she think she recognised him? Was that it?

"Reverend Roy Hope," he replied with a smile, continuing to walk away.

"Where are you staying?" Shelley asked.

Albert chose to lie. "I'm just passing through, my dear. On my way to Swansea," Albert snatched at the first Welsh place name he could think of.

Shelley let him go, watching the old man until he was out of the harbour and no longer in sight. Itching away at the back of her head, a sense of mistrust convinced her to call a friend.

Gravadlax

Glad to be away from the harbour for he'd been convinced Tanya would appear if he lingered, Albert kept his pace fast until he was two streets back into the village. Coming to Glan-Y-Wern put him in the right place geographically; news that came as a big relief, but was he really any closer to uncovering the Gastrothief?

Shelley said she had never met the earl and he never came anywhere near the boat. The boat wasn't one she saw often either. Maybe half a dozen times in the last year. A mysterious man owned it but what did that mean?

Above all else, Albert believed his next task had to be to find out more about the earl. He didn't even have a name, but believed his landlady at the bed and breakfast could supply that snippet of detail. He was on his way there now, oblivious to events occurring elsewhere in the country; events that were going to drastically shorten the time Albert had to solve the mystery of the Gastrothief.

Halfway to Thistle-Do-Me, Rex tugged at his lead, pulling his human off the path and into an area of scrubland left behind when the houses were developed around it.

He needed to find an outhouse.

Albert let him off the lead with a request that Rex not go too far. Watching to make sure his dog didn't bound into the distance, Albert relaxed when Rex started to sniff around at the undergrowth.

Killing time, Albert took out his phone. It was turned off, a state it had maintained for more than a week. He had another phone; one he bought for fifteen pounds in a supermarket when he left Cornwall. He also had Liam's phone, the Gastrothief's agent who died in Cornwall, but questioned if using it ran the risk of alerting Tanya and others to his location.

Phones could be tracked, he knew that much, and the phones of his friends and family would be monitored for any incoming transmissions – anti-terrorism laws gave all kinds of leeway to invade a person's privacy. If he switched his phone on, the police would know where he was in an instant. He found it comforting in a way - when the time came, he wouldn't even need to make a call.

He could use the supermarket phone to make calls and look things up – not that he was very good at using an internet search engine – but the people he wanted to speak with most were unavailable to him. To contact his children, or Roy, or anyone who might help him would instantly alert the police.

He'd given lots of thought to sending messages in code. If he messaged his son using the supermarket phone, the police wouldn't recognise the number, but Albert knew they would see the message for what it was – gibberish only one of his children might be able to decipher. In so doing, they would know to track the location of the phone from which the message originated, and he would be back facing the same problem using his own phone created.

Also, what could he write that would disguise who was sending the message yet make sense to the person receiving it? If he were living in a spy novel, Albert mused, his kids would be trained in a secret language dad and children developed together decades ago.

Finger resting against the power button on his phone, he knew it was too early to call anyone. He needed to get just a little closer. Another day maybe, Albert told himself. He would see Tanya if he just kept watching. Or perhaps it would be the other woman from Cornwall.

Kelly! Her name rose from the depths of his memory.

If he just kept his eyes open, he would see one of them. He could tail them and find the lair. It would be easy.

Unless he was fooling himself, a cruel voice echoed inside his head. The boat could be abandoned, never to be reclaimed. The earl could be a complete red herring. Did he really know anything?

The sound of an approaching vehicle cut through his thoughts. It was on the main road through Glan-Y-Wern which he chose to avoid in his route away from the harbour. It ran the other side of the scrubland Rex was still exploring.

"Hurry up, please, Rex," Albert called, the final word dying in his mouth as he caught sight of the vehicle.

Similar in appearance, make, and model to the green goods vehicle he saw just before lunch, passing him now was a van displaying 'Morrison's Gravadlax – suppliers to the Royal Household'.

Albert's eyes tracked the van as it passed. In the cab were two men in their early thirties. They were dressed in civilian attire, not matching uniforms one might expect to see with representatives of a high-end food company.

Out here on the Welsh coast, Albert refused to believe they were making a delivery. To his mind it was a red flag. It was exactly what he'd been looking for. In fact, the only question going through Albert's mind was whether they were arriving or leaving.

His feet were already moving, both ends of Rex's lead in his left hand.

"Rex!"

Rex lifted his head. He'd just backed into the undergrowth and didn't like to be disturbed at this point in his day. There was something in the old man's voice though. Something urgent.

"Rex!"

"All right," Rex muttered, feeling pressured to complete a task that ought not to be rushed. "All right. I heard you the first time."

He could see his human moving left to right as he continued up the hill toward their bed and breakfast.

Albert lost sight of the van behind a row of houses as it continued up the hill that led to the edge of the village and beyond. He could hear it though, and there was so little background noise, he was able to track it using a sense other than his eyes.

Regardless, Albert knew the van was going to be over the hill and out of sight long before he could call a cab and hope to give chase.

"Rex!"

Already moving, Rex bounded over a tangled bramble bush and into the street with the exuberance of a puppy.

Albert huffed, "Good boy," already getting out of breath from hurrying up the steep incline.

"Where are we going?" Rex woofed. "Do you need to go too?" He still marvelled at humanity's disgusting habit of doing their 'business' inside their dens. It just wasn't hygienic. If the old man needed to get back to their accommodation that fast, he should have just gone in the bushes next to Rex.

"I just saw a food van," Albert explained, talking to his dog like every other pet owner on the planet.

"Good thinking," Rex liked the way the old man thought. "Food would be good. It's been ages since lunch."

"I think it might be headed for the Gastrothief's lair," Albert continued, cringing at his choice of words. A master criminal's lair – it was ridiculous. No wonder the police thought he was a barmy old man. Not the safe kind who might get himself lost in a shopping mall though, more like the insane kind who would build a bomb to see if he could.

Well, lair or not ... whatever you wanted to call it, Albert reached the end of a line of houses and could see the main road again. The van was just about to crest it. Albert stopped, panting a few recovery breaths. For the first time in years, he truly wished he had a car.

He could drive and still had his license, but his reaction speed as much as anything convinced him to give up driving in his early seventies. Ok, so it was Petunia who made him stop after a third near-miss in as many months. She took over driving duties and by the time she passed, it had been five years since he was behind the wheel.

He sold their car and that was that.

Today though, he would risk it just to chase the van if he could. In theory he could steal a car. It would need to be an older model – something built in the eighties because he knew how to get into those and how to get them started. It was just one of those things he'd learned in the police - if you know how it's done, you can recognise the tools a car thief might carry and you could better advise citizens how they could protect themselves from becoming victims.

He wasn't going to steal a car though, not even if there had been an old banger sitting a few yards away with the door open and the keys in the ignition. He'd bent some laws in his pursuit of the Gastrothief, but there were limits.

The van rolled over the hill and out of sight.

Albert's eyes stayed fixed on the same spot, his shoulders rising and falling with each deep breath. It was gone. He could follow; it would take fifteen minutes at the most to get to the top of the hill. What would he see when he got there? It wouldn't be a big sign indicating 'Master Criminal's Lair' this way.

He had a map of the area in his pocket but knew without looking there was nothing much over the hill for miles.

His heartbeat was slowing, and his breathing had calmed. Racked with indecision, he was about to turn toward the bed and breakfast when the van reappeared. He only caught it from the corner of his eye.

Moving right to left, it had taken a left turn after it vanished from sight. Albert could only see the very top of the van's roof but needed no convincing that he was looking at the same vehicle.

Ripping the map from his pocket, Albert had to flip it twice before he got it the right way up. Tracing it with a finger, he found the narrow B road leading away from the main road. It skirted the coast and looked to go nowhere. Following the coast, it threaded its way along in a zigzagging loop that eventually arrived in the next town some five miles later.

Albert's heart tapped out a double thump when he realised what it could mean. Surely there could be no good reason for a truck hauling gravadlax to take a tiny coast road. Conceivably there could be a house or houses or even a hotel on that piece of coast, but there was nothing marked on his ordnance survey map.

Sucking in a deep breath through his nose, Albert knew what he was going to do.

Sent by God

Still curious about the vicar and his questions, though they seemed innocent enough, Shelley was pondering what it was about the old man that bothered her when she heard Curtis from the betting shop say something that interrupted her thoughts.

"What was that you just said?" she rudely interrupted his conversation and jumped the queue in the post office when she went around Mr and Mrs Evans to get to the front.

Gareth was behind the counter as usual; Shelley couldn't remember a day in her life when he wasn't, and both he and Curtis were looking her way when she approached.

"Here, there's a queue, you know," complained Mr Evans, ignoring his wife as she tugged on his coat sleeve to keep him from causing a scene.

Used to dealing with the rough fishermen and their proclivity for profanity, Shelley held her tongue when she swung her head to reply.

"Sorry, Mr Evans, I just need a moment. I'm not pushing in."

Curtis and Gareth were waiting for her, their conversation paused, so with Mr Evans grumbling under his breath and his wife hissing insistently, Shelley repeated her question.

"Did I just hear you talking about an old vicar? Did he have a dog with him?"

The question was aimed at Curtis, but it was Gareth who provided the answer.

"Yes. A big German Shepherd." Gareth was one of those people who would listen to what someone else knew and immediately assume a narrator's role in their story. He'd never considered why that was. At sixty-eight, he'd been working in the post office for more than fifty-five years, starting out by stacking shelves and sweeping up under his father's supervision for a little extra pocket money.

He'd never married, not because he spent his entire life in the post office and still lived at home with his ageing mother, but due almost entirely to having a permanently morose expression and outlook.

Shelley flicked her eyes at Gareth, wanting to question how it was that he knew – had the old man in the dog collar visited the post office too? Had he been asking questions there as well?

Curtis spoke before she could.

"He came into the betting shop, Shelley. He said he wanted to place a bet and was holding ..." Curtis paused, taking a second to decide what and how much he ought to reveal. "Well, he was holding a winning ticket from a bet placed months ago in Melton Mowbray."

Shelley made a face that was all question and confusion. "Melton Mowbray?"

"Ooh, they make lovely pork pies there," said Mrs Evans.

The conversation stilled for a moment; did they need to respond to her remark?

Deciding he could get away with just a smile in Mrs Evans' direction, Curtis carried on.

"The point is he had a ticket that is worth a not inconsiderable amount of money ..."

"Wait. *Had* a ticket?" Gareth cut in. Curtis had missed that part out of his story. To be fair, Shelley interrupted before he could get to it, but Gareth felt it was important enough to have led with.

Curtis' neck was getting a workout and he wasn't sure who to look at now.

46

Sticking with Shelley, he said, "Yes. That's the point really. I need to find him. He handed me the ticket and when I turned around, he vanished."

Mrs Evans asked, "What, like with a puff of smoke?"

Her husband, long bored with his wife's nagging and incessant need to ask questions, said, "Why would he vanish in a puff of smoke, you daft old bag?"

Reacting as if slapped, Mrs Evans gasped and stepped a half pace away. Facing her husband she knew well enough that such a public display of disrespect had to be quashed.

With a voice like thunder, she growled, "Eric Evans."

Eric knew he'd gone too far. Visions of cold meals he had to prepare himself swam into his brain.

"Now don't let's get excited, dear."

"Don't you 'dear' me. You just called me a daft old bag!" Her hands were heading to her hips. She might be eighty-three years old, but she wasn't about to be disrespected by anyone. Least of all her own husband. "Just you wait until I get you home!" She stormed from the shop, offering her last comment as a demand that he follow.

Eric twisted to offer a weak smile to the other people in the post office. Shelley, Curtis, and Gareth looked his way, but said nothing, collectively thinking he probably deserved whatever he had coming.

"We'll … um. We'll be back in a minute," he rolled his eyes in a way that he believed would make it look like his wife was making a lot of fuss about nothing, though he refrained from his desire to say, 'Women?' in a tone that would suggest they were the best and worst of a man's life.

Silence fell inside the shop at Mr Evan's departure, but only for a moment.

With a shake of her head to clear it, Shelley retraced a few mental steps to pick up where she left off.

"The vicar came into the betting shop to collect a bet worth a fortune, but left before collecting it?"

Curtis nodded. "That's right. Now my boss wants me to find him." Okay, so that wasn't strictly true and Curtis was still waiting for the PR person to call him. When he left the shop in the questionable hands of the next senior person, Russel, Curtis told himself it was prudent to know where to find the old vicar. Otherwise, they might call to arrange a publicity event or some such only to discover Curtis had let the winner slip through his fingers. He was not going to be the one without a chair when the music stopped, things went wrong, and they were looking for someone to blame. Also, Curtis was just plain curious.

"Why?"

"Why find him? Well, because he's won a lot of money," Curtis explained slowly as if he were speaking to someone particularly dense.

"Yes, but surely not having to pay him is a good thing?"

"How much money are we talking about?" asked Gareth, already wondering if they could keep it all quiet, collect the winnings and divide it between those who knew i.e. the three people currently discussing the subject.

"What money?" asked Morty Byers as he came through the post office door. "Here, I just bumped into old Mr and Mrs Evans in the street outside. Had to break them up," he revealed with a snigger. "Mrs Evans was hitting him with her handbag. Anyway, what money? What are we talking about?"

Shelley got in first, but she didn't answer Morty, she asked a question.

"Have you seen an old vicar out walking a giant German Shepherd?"

Morty's eyebrows danced a little jig as he looked from Shelley to Gareth and onto Curtis. He was trying to decipher the question and hoping one of the fellas would tell him what it meant.

"Um, no," he ventured, still unsure whether the question was serious or the leading line of a joke.

"He's wearing a big parka coat," Shelley pressed Morty's memory.

Able to see the man had no idea what Shelley was talking about, Curtis said, "He's a visitor to the village, Morty. No one special."

"No one special?" Gareth wasn't about to lose sight of the money. "You just said he handed over the betting stub worth a fortune and walked away."

Morty only popped in to get some digestive biscuits to go with his next cup of tea. They went forgotten though as he came close to listen.

"You know what I reckon?" Gareth had lowered his voice to a conspiratorial whisper. "That old vicar left the winning betting stub here on purpose." He checked to make sure everyone was listening. "He wants us to have it," he nodded his head as he spoke in the hope they would all nod along in agreement. "We can claim the money and split it between us." He risked a glance at the door and thought about locking it before anyone else could come in.

A little startled by the unexpected post office clerk's suggestion, Curtis said, "Sorry, we cannot do that."

"Why not?" asked Morty who was also quite interested in an unexpected windfall.

"Well, for a start because we wouldn't get away with it. I already informed head office and given that the amount we are talking about is quite substantial ..."

"How much?" Shelley asked.

Curtis was careful to repeat himself. "Substantial. You might get away walking in with someone else's betting slip when it's just a tenner being won. This chap will get his face in the papers."

"So who is he?" asked Gareth. "If he's not a charitable philanthropist sent by God to help us in our time of need?" He wasn't letting go of his fantasy without a fight.

Shelley screwed up her face in disbelief, "What time of need? Gareth you run this place and still live with your mum. Everyone knows you're loaded."

Gareth fell silent, but the question about the old vicar's identity refused to go away. Shelley told the guys about the questions he'd been asking, about the yacht and about the old stately home and the earl.

As mystery gave way to enigma, the group agreed to start quietly asking around. If the old man was staying in the village it had to be with a relative or in one of the three bed and breakfasts Glan-Y-Wern could boast. Someone would know where he was staying.

When everyone but Gareth filed from the shop, Morty's digestive biscuits forgotten on the shelf, they walked past a rack of papers and magazines. If just one of them had picked up a copy of The Independent Enquirer, they might have found the article showing a very familiar face and a story that would have made their toes curl.

Unspoiled View

The ground didn't flatten out when he reached the crest of the hill as Albert hoped it might. He knew that before he got there, of course, catching sight of the second rise before he reached the top of the first. A check of the map would have revealed the contour lines, but it was only when he discovered there was still more 'up' that he thought to examine the item clutched in his spare hand.

His other hand held Rex's lead. They were tracking along the side of a main road. Not intended for pedestrians, no pavement skirted it and a wire fence to keep sheep in their field prevented man and dog from getting more than a foot off the tarmac. Keeping his dog close by his side in case more traffic came their way, Albert breathed a sigh of relief when the sheep field gave way to open countryside.

The van and its load of gravadlax were long gone. However, the map showed there really wasn't anywhere it could have gone other than along the narrow road skirting the coast. Cutting across the low, scrubby grass, Albert shortened his route to arrive on the dark grey tarmac once more.

The narrow B road cut a line toward what looked like the end of the world from his angle. Somewhere out of sight it would turn to follow the land which dropped off abruptly into the sea according to the map. Albert stared at it once more, scrutinising the lines showing gradient and near featureless land sandwiched between the cliffs and the main road carving north across Wales.

There really was nothing between his current position and the next village some five miles away. He looked but could not see a stately home anywhere. However, further inland where the land gave way to mountains in the distance, there were plentiful clumps of trees that could easily hide such a grand building.

Staring across the barren countryside, he asked, "Fancy a long walk?"

Rex didn't exactly understand the question. He knew the word 'walk' but they were already doing that. His human's behaviour could be best described as inexplicable on a regular basis, so today was no different and he accepted it without comment.

He wanted to look for Tanya; she deserved to be chased and bitten. It could wait though, his desire for justice would always come second behind his *need* to protect the old man. He could do that better by sticking close by his human's side.

A rabbit's head popped up on the other side of the road. Instinctively, Rex's feet spasmed, his brain hardwired to send him after it. He knew they were around, of course; their scent was everywhere, but tempting though they were, he managed to control his urge to give chase just before Albert shortened his lead.

"No bunnies, Rex," Albert chided. Now was not the time to lose his dog.

Forging ahead and crossing the road, Albert steered Rex on a route that would cut a small amount of distance off their journey. He planned to walk all the way to the next village if that was what it took. Since the map showed nothing, he was interested to see if there was anything here.

Why else would the gravadlax van have come this way?

Estimating that it would take no more than two hours to cover the five miles if indeed he walked all the way without spotting something worthy of a closer look, Albert knew he would be cutting it fine to get there before the sun set.

It was already dipping, the days short as autumn thought about yielding to winter. His eyes didn't work very well in the dark – another reason why he gave up driving – and worried he might stumble and fall on the uneven ground, he kept the road in sight.

The land climbed another dozen or so yards which took a mile to do, so the incline went unnoticed. Regardless, Albert's hips and knees began to ache, a tax he accepted before setting off.

About thirty minutes into their walk, Albert reached a high point. Scanning in every direction he could see Glan-Y-Wern to the southeast and the next village to the northwest. The name escaped him. He'd seen it on a signpost, and it was one of those wonderful Welsh ones with consonants for vowels so he wouldn't be able to say it even if he could remember what it was.

Gorse bushes and a few short trees devoid of leaves in deference to the time of year broke up the immediate landscape, but apart from the two villages and a forest a mile or more away in the distance to the east, there was nothing within walking distance in any direction.

With a sigh to replace the curse words Albert wanted to employ, he took a moment to feel sorry for himself again. He wasn't the kind of person who would pray for God's help in such circumstances. Not due to a lack of faith, but because he believed God didn't work that way. Albert got himself into this mess - he couldn't pray his way out of it.

There was nothing here. Not visibly anyway. What happened to the gravadlax truck? Who could guess? Albert surmised the driver chose to take a scenic route. He could have been on his way to a restaurant or hotel in the unpronounceable village ahead. Maybe there were roadworks on the main road and the driver knew how to avoid them.

Many reasons could be behind the delivery van's seemingly strange choice of route, and most were more believable than Albert's wild theory that it had been stolen.

Assassin for Hire

Tanya clicked the mouse and pressed return. How she came to be making entries on a spreadsheet was not a subject she wanted to explore. A week ago at this time she was just arriving in Cornwall and happy to be on the hunt for Albert Smith and his damned dog.

She would never openly admit that she liked killing people, not even to herself. Deep inside though, she knew it was true. It gave her power. The power to determine if a person lived or died. Responsible for twelve deaths, she wasn't a murderer, she was an assassin for hire.

It was a completely different thing, and no one would ever convince her otherwise.

Tanya would never just kill a person, not unless they got in her way or annoyed her. Being paid to kill people though, that was okay. Better than okay, in fact.

Somehow though, working for the earl and worming her way into his confidence so she could orchestrate her own missions, she became a victim of her own success. Not that she always succeeded.

Failing to remove Albert Smith in Cornwall stung. She had the chance to kill him more than once. Why hadn't she just pulled the trigger? It wasn't a hard question to answer: she wanted to bring him back to the earl. Tanya expected to succeed where others had failed.

Returning minus yet another of the earl's agents when they lost Liam, and minus the food, drink, and people the team were sent to collect, the mission to Cornwall was an abject failure. Thankfully, pasties and cider were assigned to Kelly and Liam and the failure was theirs, not Tanya's. She made sure the earl knew they were also to blame for Albert Smith's continued existence.

In the aftermath of their escape from the disaster in Looe, Albert Smith vanished. His presence brought the police to the seaside town in droves, forcing Tanya to abandon any last vestige of hope that she could catch him.

He was out there somewhere now. Albert Smith couldn't go home – Tanya wasn't the only person looking for the old man, the authorities were too, yet the wily old goat was able to elude them and everyone else.

Pushing away from the desk and the stupid spreadsheet she was somehow now responsible for completing, Tanya stood and stretched. The gravadlax was in and accounted for; there were people loading it into the freezers now. Mike and Ian's successful hijacking of the delivery van cost the real driver his life. They would be heading out again within the hour, heading north to Kendal for mint cake, a strange delicacy Tanya despised.

The earl had a list of all the things he wanted. Spices, flavours ... plants that would continue to produce fresh fruit or whatever, the earl wanted it all. His original approach had been cautious, sending his employees – career criminals like Tanya – to make the collections. He could have bought the things he wanted, but refused to. He believed that if anyone found out what he was doing, found out about his refuge from the impending global apocalypse, a stampede would result.

The crazy fat man wanted his location to remain secret from the world. Buying a lifetime supply of Stilton cheese would cause comment and interest he refused to risk.

The cautious plan got kicked into touch after Cornwall. To Tanya, Albert Smith was a strange conundrum. One could easily believe he was working for someone else; the tenacious old dog kept turning up like a shark following a blood trail. How many times had he interrupted one of the earl's collections?

Too many, that was for sure. Often enough that some of the other teams were using him as an excuse when they ran into any trouble.

But it wasn't the retired detective that had the Earl so spooked. He wanted everything done as quickly as possible. It was the recent news coverage of 'The Gastrothief'. She smirked at the name; it was so ridiculous. It did fit though.

Almost overnight when the article was first published, a social media movement evolved and then went viral. Everyone was talking about Albert Smith and there were hundreds of people claiming to have seen him. As a tactic to defeat the police in their desire to apprehend the old man, it was ingenious, but Tanya doubted that was ever the intention.

Whatever they did hope to achieve, it resulted in panic on the part of her boss. The earl begged her to help wrap up his collections as swiftly as possible. He'd even cut down his list of collections, agonising over which of his favourite foods he could learn to live without.

There were teams out all over, making dozens of final collections over the next two days. That was how she came to be the one overseeing it all. Earning the earl's trust hadn't exactly backfired; he offered her a fat sum when she initially resisted. However, it wasn't what she wanted to do.

Earl Bacon planned to close the door and seal himself inside in three days' time. Her time with him had been the most lucrative of her life, but all good things come to an end, and she was ready for a vacation. She had Napoli in her sights and enough money in her bank to live like a queen.

She didn't need to work again for years if she so chose, but knew her feet would begin to itch after a few weeks of doing nothing.

Leaving the office to check the gravadlax had all been offloaded and stored, she tried very hard to focus on the job in hand. Images of Albert Smith's face kept surfacing though. She wasn't used to failing and it was keeping her awake at night.

Three days, she told herself. She could do this for three days. Fleece the earl for every penny she could and slip out moments after he made the final transfer to her account. He could lock himself and his prisoners inside as he planned, and Tanya would never give them another thought. He had loyal followers among his staff who were dumb enough to buy into his premonitions of doom. One of them could take over once she was safely somewhere else.

And as for Albert Smith and his dog ... well, if she ever saw them again, she would kill them both without the slightest hesitation.

Rising Panic

Almost an hour passed without a single car or van passing along the narrow coast road. Albert's earlier concerns about letting Rex off the lead dissolved and setting his dog free to wander made negotiating the rough terrain easier for Albert's aging body.

Rex bounded here and there, doing his best to ignore the rabbits he could see in every direction. They were everywhere, the hoppity, little furballs constantly triggering a message to give chase.

"Must not chase bunnies," Rex repeated a mantra. His human said it a dozen times before he unclipped the lead and again every time he caught Rex eyeing them. It was the tails as much as it was anything. The white underfur flicked into the air as they darted away like a strobe light calling him to follow.

With the exception of the ever-tempting rabbits, Rex was having as good a time as any dog could. Out in the countryside on a dry day with miles and miles of open land in which he could stretch his legs. Bunnies to chase if his human got distracted … what more could he ask for?

An eternally replenishing open pot of gravy bones, obviously. Sticking within the bounds of reality though, Rex was content with his lot.

His nose led him here and there, but unlike the villages and towns he more frequently explored, there wasn't a whole lot to smell. The local fauna left their scents behind, but it was almost exclusively rabbits. He'd crossed the path of a fox a few minutes ago, but the scent it left was two days old.

No humans had been out this way. It wasn't just his sense of smell carrying that message, his eyes agreed. The lack of litter and undisturbed undergrowth told the same story.

It was due to this fact that the sudden and unexpected aroma of cooking meat came as a shock. Somewhere nearby a piece of beef was being slow cooked. Circling to find a direction, Rex began to track.

Bay leaves, thyme, salt, pepper, and other spices clung to the air, mingling with the unmistakeable perfume of the meat as it cooked slowly in a meaty broth. Drawn like a cat to a delicate and precious ornament, Rex had no power to resist.

Albert saw Rex take a detour. Out here in the open countryside, he saw no reason to call him back. The dog could wander fifty yards away without Albert becoming concerned - Rex would come back when he was called.

They were halfway to the next village now. There he would catch a bus or a taxi back to Glan-Y-Wern, annoyed that his lengthy walk netted no result. He wasn't there yet though, he countered, arguing with himself. There was still time to make a discovery.

Positive thinking was one thing. The brutal truth was another, and despite a determination to not feel defeated, Albert's faith had flagged, withered and died more than half an hour ago. It hadn't exactly been healthy when he started. There was nothing here. Anyone could see that. He was going to walk all the way to the next village, wasting the bulk of his afternoon and getting sore for the heck of it.

Rex would be happy. Checking to his left to make sure his dog hadn't wandered too far, he paused when there was no sign of him. Swivelling his body to face the direction he'd last seen Rex, Albert told himself to remain calm.

With two fingers in his mouth, he whistled.

"Rex? Rex, come on boy."

He got no answer either. He was just behind a bush, surely. Five more seconds ticked by.

"Rex! Rex, where are you?"

A frown formed to accompany the itch of worry now tickling his gut. There wasn't anything here the dog could hide behind. A hole perhaps. Not a badger warren, Rex was a German Shepherd not a dachshund; he wouldn't fit in the burrow of any creature native to the UK.

"Rex!" Albert crossed the scrubland, quickly arriving at the last place he'd seen the dog. There was no sign of him.

A calming breath to counteract the rising panic did little to quell the urgent alarm bells in his head. Rex hadn't been taken by anyone, but he could have run off.

"Rex!"

Underground

Rex couldn't hear Albert calling for him. Not because he was unconscious or temporarily deaf. No, the reason his human's ever more urgent shouts were not finding their target was the distance now between them and the insulation dampening out the background noise.

Following his nose, Rex had come to a collection of craggy boulders. Lined with sediment and covered in lichen, they failed to match the land around them which was entirely devoid of such rocks.

Oblivious to the strangeness of the geology, Rex knew the meaty scent emanated from within the rocky mound. After pausing to leave his mark, Rex walked around the rocks. They were half as high again as his shoulders, forcing him to bounce onto his hind legs to see over the top.

There was nothing to see. The rocks were bunched together leaving few gaps.

Until Rex reached the other side. There he found a triangular gap at the bottom where one rock rested against another. The source of the smell lay within. With globs of saliva now hanging from his jowls, it would have taken a titanic force to prevent the German Shepherd from exploring further.

Edging forward on his belly, he pushed between the rocks.

A human would have been shocked to find a stainless-steel grate on the ground inside the rocks. A human would have questioned what on earth it could be doing there and might have proceeded to investigate.

Rex did none of that. Led by his nose which was being powered along by his stomach, Rex clambered onto the steel grate. Warm air rose from it carrying the rich scent of beef broth. When the grate shifted and flipped, there was nothing Rex could do to prevent his fall.

Had Albert been closer, he might have heard his dog's small squeal of alarm, but Albert was still fifty yards away at the time and the sound Rex gave was instantly lost to the breeze outside.

Mercifully, he was falling through a ventilation pipe, a steel cylinder that angled down through the earth rather than plummeting perpendicular to the surface. Hurtling face first into the dark, Rex tried to use his front paws to slow his descent. They had little effect.

His fall lasted less than two seconds, during which time he descended almost a hundred feet. At the bottom of the chute, the pipe spat him into a square channel with a bump that knocked the wind from his chest.

He needed a moment to recover, but only a second to assess that he was unharmed. Once he had his breath back, Rex stood up. Or, at least, he tried to.

The roof of the ventilation shaft was several inches too short for his frame, so his back hit the ceiling before his legs were fully extended.

Rex laid back down to think.

The meaty odour was coming from behind him – the pipe he fell down connected to a shaft that ran in both directions. There wasn't enough room to turn around, so with no choice in the matter, Rex assumed an awkward crouching position and began to make his way through the steel box.

The space was utterly devoid of light, a sensation that might have been close to overwhelming for a human. For a dog, it proved to be a little disorienting, yet of minor concern as his nose told him all there was to know.

Rats had been in the shaft. Not where he was, but further down; their scent was a background note, but undeniable. The food smell was there too and to Rex that meant there had to be people.

The cramped confines of the ventilation shaft meant he needed to lie down to rest his legs every minute or so, but he pushed on, always in one direction until he came to a connecting shaft.

Now faced with a choice, Rex sniffed both paths. One carried a faint trace of sea water. Setting off again, he aimed his nose that way.

Hopelessly Searching

I t was thirty minutes into Albert's increasingly worried search that he finally chanced upon the rocks. Out of breath from shouting his dog's name, and increasingly fatigued, he needed a place to rest. The rocks presented a dry place to perch his backside and a vantage point from which he could gain a better view across the surrounding countryside once he felt up to climbing them.

The daylight had already begun to fade, the late autumn sun heading for the horizon many hours earlier than it would in the summer. Albert knew darkness would make his search even harder while simultaneously heightening his chances of a sprained ankle or worse.

The terrain was treacherous; pocked with rabbit holes and low-lying scrub that was easy to avoid in the daylight but would be nigh impossible to see once the last of the sun's rays lost their fight to hold onto this half of the world. Adding to the problem, the sky above was coated in cloud, eliminating any hope the moon might come to his rescue.

Massaging his knees one after the other, Albert talked to himself. "Where are you, dog?" It was unusual for Rex to run off. Ok sure, the headstrong German Shepherd would pelt into the distance without a second thought if he had someone to chase, but out here in the open his disappearance was incongruous.

Had Rex run back to their bed and breakfast? Albert was certain he would have been able to spot him bounding into the distance. Had he fallen into a hole? That had been Albert's first concern. For all he knew there were crevasses this close to the coast. Half an hour of searching revealed nothing though, and they would be marked on his map, surely.

So what did that leave?

Feeling somewhat rested and ready to renew his search with a wider circumference, Albert was about to clamber onto the rocks when he caught a whiff of the same beefy smell Rex was unable to resist.

The smell stopped him dead in his tracks, his whole body freezing for a second to analyse the scent. However, unlike his dog, who could dismantle the flavour profile, reducing it to individual components, Albert simply questioned how it was that he could smell food.

He stayed like that for half a minute, running different scenarios through his head. There was something fishy about the food smell this far from civilisation. Unable to trace a source in the same manner Rex had, Albert could form no conclusion other than to dismiss it as unconnected to his dog's disappearing act.

"Okay, pup," Albert heaved himself onto the rocks and stood up his full height. "Wherever you are, I'm not leaving here without you. If you could please make your location known before I die from exposure, I would appreciate it."

Sucking in a lungful of air, he shouted Rex's name again, turning each time to bellow in a different direction. Once he'd completed a full circle and there was still no sign of his dog, he carefully lowered himself back to the ground level and set off walking again.

Dogs don't just vanish; Rex was here somewhere.

Scent of a Woman

Rex was getting thoroughly bored with the ventilation shaft. Shuffling in the hunched manner the low ceiling enforced, for the first time in his life he found himself wishing he had been born a terrier. Or a spaniel. Any breed would do, just so long as he could stretch his legs and stand.

More than an hour into his exploration, it taking so long because he needed longer and longer rest periods to alleviate the cramping in his legs, Rex discerned a dim glow ahead. The scents reaching his nose hadn't changed much since he landed at the bottom of the chute, but to accompany the glow, Rex detected the scent of a human.

It was a male; the scent of his sweat being all Rex needed to tell the difference. He wore a familiar cologne; one Rex recognised but could not name, and was chewing spearmint gum.

Edging ever forward, and refusing to rest now though his muscles protested, the dim glow grew brighter. And brighter.

Flooded with relief, Rex saw the shaft ended ahead. The light was coming through a slatted panel, not dissimilar from that which gave way beneath him when he ventured under the rocks. The man Rex could smell was in the room ahead, and he was singing along to music playing on the radio.

Rex didn't know that the man was offkey and wouldn't have cared. To his ears, the sound of a human singing was like a choir of angels. It meant rescue was at hand. He could bark to draw attention, certain he would be heard and believing more humans would come to help the stricken hound.

Humans were like that – they wanted to help animals when they saw them in distress.

However, just as Rex was coming to the end of the tunnel, a new scent tickled his nose.

A new scent that was an old scent. A familiar scent. The scent of a woman he needed to bite.

"Hey, what's taking so long?" Tanya's voice echoed in the room below.

Rex couldn't see her. Not yet. His hackles rose though, and his lips drew back to expose his teeth. Fighting hard to suppress the desire to growl and bark, he stilled his body to listen.

The man mumbled something in reply, got a terse response and left with Tanya, their footsteps receding until Rex could hear only the gentle hum of a motor somewhere.

Tanya.

Rex gave himself a moment to think. His natural reaction was to exit the shaft with a burst of energy and launch an attack before she knew what was happening or had the slightest chance to react. He doubted, however, that his legs would work the way he wanted them to. He needed to walk around for a while and stretch out his back.

Not only that, Rex knew not to underestimate Tanya. Like his own human, she was tenacious and capable. Few other humans had escaped him when he chose to give chase, yet she remained at large, and she was generally armed.

Heck, she'd come closer to ending him than the other way around. On more than one occasion, Rex reflected.

There was still no sound coming from whatever was beyond the slatted panel, so seizing the opportunity this presented, Rex shuffled/crawled until his nose touched it and he could see what was on the other side.

The ventilation shaft, fitted by the engineers who designed and built the underground chamber in secret, pumped air in and out of the Earl's lair through a series of filters and scrubbers. The shaft through which Rex gained entry was one of four providing air to the population living below ground. It terminated in one of the kitchens, specifically the Earl's kitchen for his food was stored, prepared, and managed separately from that which was given to everyone else.

Entering high on a wall, there was a refrigerator just two feet beneath the hole.

Turning his head to squint through the holes with one eye, Rex could see his way into the room. All he had to do was get past the panel currently blocking the way.

He pushed it with the crown of his head. Just like the one he fell through, it hinged from one edge – in this case, the top edge.

It took a fair amount of pressure to get it to move, but it wasn't as though Rex had many choices. He was going through the panel or staying in the shaft until he starved to death. Barking was no longer an option – there was too much danger that Tanya would appear.

With the vent panel resting on his face, Rex slid carefully out of the shaft. His front legs reached down, pawing the air as they tried to get to the top of the industrial sized refrigerator. It was further than he first estimated. By the time his body was balanced on the cusp of falling, his paws were still a foot or more from the surface below.

Scrabbling to find purchase on the slick steel with his back paws, Rex leaned out just a little further.

And overbalanced.

A woof of horror burst from his throat when he toppled. It could be easily translated, but would then be unprintable, so we'll leave it as a woof for the sake of decorum.

His front paws hit the top of the fridge and skidded toward the front edge. His bum plopped out of the shaft, the panel swinging shut behind it with a clang.

The noise echoed through the room, but it was the least of Rex's concerns. His back end had been doing the bulk of the work for the last hour and was screaming to be permitted to rest. He needed it to operate though. If his back legs couldn't fire when they touched down, he was going to fall right over the edge to the cold, black tile a further seven feet below.

And that was going to hurt.

Enigma

A little more than a mile and a half from Rex's current location, a gang of villagers had congregated to discuss the newcomer in their midst. The village pub, the only one remaining of three Glan-Y-Wern could boast in the seventies, enjoyed the surprising boom in customers.

The Old Seamaster on the seafront opposite the harbour knew its clientele well and rarely saw anyone new walking through the doors. It survived by being staffed entirely by Glynn Travis and his wife Sally. He worked a fishing boat from the crack of dawn until just around noon, sneaking in a nap once he'd eaten to then be able to make it through to last orders without falling asleep on the bar.

The pub just about covered its costs and paid them a meagre wage on a bad month. In the summer, when a few day trippers could be expected, and in the run up to Christmas, they could actually make a half decent amount of profit.

However, a full crowd and standing room only at half past five on a Saturday? Glynn had never seen the like. He and Sally couldn't pull pints fast enough. Glynn had a moment of panic when he thought they might not have enough stock – what could be worse than running out of beer when they had a glut of customers?

Thankfully, it was always Sally who managed the inventory, and they had plenty of everything due to a delivery from the brewery just two days ago.

Neither Glynn nor Sally cared what was behind the sudden rush of locals needing to be part of the action, but it wasn't like they could avoid the topic being discussed – it was being shouted and argued by everyone.

"He could be an old assassin coming out of retirement for one last job," suggested Ian Peck, a man who once fancied himself as a thriller novelist. "Think about it," he insisted to the unspoken ridicule etched into the faces of everyone who'd heard what he said. "Where else could he enjoy such anonymity? We're at the end of the world here." He gasped when a new thought struck. "I bet he's not even a real vicar. It could be his nickname, like that's what the police or Interpol and what-have-you called him because they never found out who he was. I bet he's always left a calling card on his victims. A bible or a rosary maybe." Ian moved to the village when his wife kicked him out more than ten years ago. It was supposed to be a temporary arrangement until he got himself sorted out, but the back bedroom he rented proved to be adequate to his needs and he'd stayed.

Partly it was the joy of moving to a new place where no one knew him, and he could craft a history that better reflected the life he felt he ought to have had. Three weeks in the Territorial Army in his twenties became a secret military past he didn't dare talk about, except in hints and whispers he would then refuse to embellish.

Ignoring him, Shelley said, "Someone must know where he is staying. What's the latest on Agnes?"

Agnes Dalgleish lived in Rose House and was reputed to be older than some of the rocks on which the town was built. No one knew when she was born but everyone agreed she was Glan-Y-Wern's oldest resident.

"No answer," replied Carl Whyman, her neighbour. "I'll pop around and knock on the door when I've finished this pint. Like I said earlier though, I don't think she has any residents at the moment."

Almost a quarter of the villagers were assembled in the tiny pub which was bursting at the seams and a fire marshall's nightmare. Word of a mysterious stranger in their midst had spread fast, messages passing from phone to phone and by word of mouth. Not to the under twenties, you understand. The teens merely rolled their eyes at the sad antics their parents were displaying, and the children never even heard what was being said.

It was the money as much as anything that got them all stirred up. Not a lot happened in Glan-Y-Wern.

Ever.

Now they had an old man who might or might not be a vicar, but could equally be a former hitman if anyone cared to heed Ian Peck's warnings. He was worth a huge sum of money, billions possibly, the Chinese whisper effect claimed. Curtis refused to be drawn on the subject. He was in the pub though, abandoning any thoughts of returning to work when an innocent question aimed at the post office manager exploded into a full-scale, village-wide investigation.

Few had noticed the man in question though Pamela from the chip shop claimed to have served him at lunch today.

"He ordered a large bag of chips and shared it with his dog," she mumbled around a gin and tonic.

Curtis was telling himself to be pleased with all the attention – it was his attention, he'd already decided. The furore was all about the aa, not about the old man, and people were asking questions. Specific questions specifically about the bet and how to specifically replicate it.

He wasn't a betting man - a subject he kept quiet – but Curtis Jones was willing to bet there would be a queue outside his shop tomorrow. Everyone who approached him got a nod and a wink to accompany his advice that 'he would help them gamble responsibly' when they came to the shop.

That was all well and good but where was the old man? Vicar or not - Curtis saw no reason to doubt the dog collar - he needed to be found. Now that the betting slip was locked in the filing cabinet at the shop, and the owner of the company had been informed, Curtis knew he was going to have to produce him.

The PR person or people were yet to call, but they would.

Thinking aloud, he said, "If he's not staying with Agnes, and we know he isn't here," the pub was the third location offering accommodation which had acted as a nice excuse to all meet there, "then he must be with Malory and Joshua in Thistle-Do-Me."

His observation halted most conversation in the bar.

"They're not answering the phone," Shelley highlighted.

Ian Peck suggested, "We should go there. Armed though, just in case I'm right."

Shelley offered Ian a withering look that had no impact on his spy novel ideas whatsoever.

"We *should* go there," she agreed. "Who's in?"

Expecting an immediate roar of approval and a show of hands, Shelley was disappointed to watch shuffling feet and eyes avoiding hers.

Exasperated, she locked eyes with Ian again. "It was your idea!"

Cheeks reddening, Ian mumbled, "Absolutely. I'll be happy to lead the expedition, obviously. As a former military man, I suppose it only makes sense that I act as the tip of the spear so to speak."

"He's eighty if he's a day, Ian," Shelley snapped. "And he's not a hitman for goodness sake."

"Either way, I've just got this pint," Ian argued weakly. "Perhaps we can delay our departure until I've finished it?"

Shelley was about to argue, but stopped when she remembered that a fresh Guinness had only just been pressed into her hand.

Letting the matter drop for now, she promised herself they would go when they finished their drinks.

Underground Evasion

Having successfully negotiated his way into the earl's kitchen, Rex waited atop the refrigerator until his legs felt ready to perform athletic feats. Seven feet up there was no easy way down. He could jump straight down to the floor below - his legs could take it - but the shine on the tile made Rex question if his paws would skid and slide the instant they made contact.

If he jumped, he would be risking a broken leg or worse. A better solution was to jump across to another machine that was a foot shorter than the one he now stood upon. It was five feet away, a distance he could easily cover.

With a run up.

Less easy from a standing start.

Weighing up his options, Rex didn't like any of them, but now was not the time to dally, so he bunched his muscles, breathed in slowly, let half of it go, and launched into space.

Had there been anyone nearby, they would have heard the oversized German Shepherd slam into the side of the freezer to shunt it three inches sideways. His back paws had failed to grip the slick top surface of the refrigerator when he pushed off, so his leap of faith carried him barely two thirds of the distance required.

His face smacked into the unforgiving side of the appliance whereupon he slid southward until he got his paws arranged to shove away. Twisting in mid-air, Rex performed a manoeuvre a cat would be proud of to land on his paws, uninjured save for a sore gum.

He was down, that was the important thing. His human was back at the surface; Rex doubted the old man would follow even if he was able to. That was a concern and a problem at the same time. Right now though, Rex needed to get his bearings and find a way out.

His nose reminded him of the smell that drew him here in the first place – '*Perhaps a small snack to rejuvenate my energy levels,*' Rex thought to himself, grinning a doggy grin at the images playing in his head.

There was food here; that was for certain. Finding it wouldn't be too hard. The question, Rex decided, was whether he should look for Tanya or avoid her? He was on her turf. In a canine world that meant something. However, it only really applied to dogs, and he could smell no other canines in his vicinity.

Pausing to mark the edge of the freezer, Rex trotted gamely out through an open door and into a brightly lit corridor.

The scents assailing his nostrils were easy enough to identify, but no less confusing because he knew what they were. If anything, the confluence of so many smells *was* the point of confusion.

He was underground; the background odour of damp earth was everywhere. He could also smell the sea which made no sense. There were people here, which he knew already, but sniffing deeply and closing his eyes to better analyse what he could smell, Rex was able to pick out dozens of different people. Men, women, and children as if he had fetched upon a small community.

The food smells were another source of wonder. Pies, cured meats, fermenting alcohol ... fish.

Fish.

Rex's eyes snapped open. It wasn't just fish he could smell, it was smoked fish. The exact same smoked fish scent he encountered in Arbroath and deep within the grease-laden smoke hid the scent of a man he knew.

Rex wasn't sure what that meant; he was a little woolly on the concept of kidnap. However, adding Tanya's presence to the equation, and remembering that his human stayed in Arbroath trying to find the missing man after he vanished, Rex concluded there was enough reason to seek the man out.

He had to rack his canine brain to remember the human's name: Argyll.

Setting off to track the scent to its source, he made sure to stick to the shadows where possible. There were humans nearby, but were they friendly? Tanya had moved away; her individual smell was fading, but could he trust anyone else?

Opting to stay out of sight until he found Argyll – a man he did trust – Rex froze when he heard footsteps coming his way. His nose assured him it wasn't Tanya; he would settle the score with her later, but he was effectively trapped in a corridor and his only escape route was back to the room he first landed in.

Turning about, he spotted a door to his left. A nudge with his head confirmed it was locked. Quickening his pace to stay ahead of the as yet unseen humans coming his way, Rex tried another door and another. None yielded to his skull.

With nothing else for it, he ran back to the kitchen/food prep area. His progress stymied, Rex forced himself to be calm – they would pass, and he would be free to try again.

What if they didn't pass though?

The footsteps were still coming his way. Two sets of them. Two men, his nose confirmed with a jolt of alarm because one of the men was the one Rex spotted from the ventilation shaft! The man came from this room, leaving when Tanya arrived.

Now he was coming back!

Rex squared his paws, setting his stance and bunching his muscles so he felt ready to leap. If in doubt attack, right? The opportunity to sneak about the place and find Argyll would be gone, but faced with no choice, he would do what was necessary and make the rest up as he went along.

His top lip curled back to show his teeth, but he kept his growl inside, waiting to surprise the men when they came through the door.

With a few seconds until they would arrive, Rex's eyes flicked left and right to check his surroundings - he wanted to have the layout of the room set in his mind. Spying a stainless-steel table to his right, Rex realised he could attack the men from face height if he mounted it. There was time.

However, when he shifted position, he spotted something that he'd somehow missed until now: a door.

There was another door in the room. Set into the back wall, it wasn't one with a handle his paws would struggle to turn or twist, but a push bar set in the centre at Rex's head height. An emergency exit was just what Rex needed.

With no idea where it led and no time to waste, he bounded across the room and jumped to place his front paws on the bar. It gave and he tumbled through.

Eat, Drink, and be Merry

Rex half fell, half bounced into the space beyond the door with the push-bar, skidding to a halt on the other side with his eyes so wide the orbs threatened to fall out. A dog would never say 'I couldn't believe my eyes'. For them seeing is a sense that should be relied on only rarely. Rex, however, could not believe his nose.

For a human experiencing the same, they might imagine a choir of angels singing from on high or a magical, ephemeral, giant starlit finger coming down from heaven while a voice whispers, 'It's your turn.'

The push-bar door swung closed behind Rex's tail with a click, the oil-pressured actuator mounted at the top ensuring it stayed closed to keep the space within cool.

Unable to convince his paws to move, Rex simply stared. The room was roughly five yards by eight with a ceiling some three yards above his head. The dimensions were lost on the dog though; all he could see was the food.

Hung from meat hooks, cured whole hams and lengths of sausage from two dozen different nations competed for space next to shelves of cheeses. The Gastrothief's cold store, chilled to a cool six degrees centigrade, held a lifetime supply of meats and cheeses from around the world. There were pastries too; pies and puddings defrosted in readiness for the earl's meals over the next few days.

A line of drool from either side of Rex's open mouth lost their individual fights against the ravages of gravity, sploshing to the ground next to his front paws. It snapped him from the daydream he'd maintained in case he awoke to find that was all it had ever been.

Lifting his back end from the cold stone tile, he licked his lips and wondered what to sample first. Unaware that he was locked in with no way of getting out and a distinct chance he might suffer hypothermia from the controlled cold, Rex would not have cared if he had. If the earl's chef opened the door now, Rex would have closed it again keeping himself on the inside.

Barely able to contain himself, Rex sniffed his way along one of the counters. They were waist high for a human, head height for him, but there wasn't a piece of food in the entire room that Rex wouldn't be able to get to.

Starting with an Iberico ham, a specialty of Spain, Rex pulled it from the hook using his body weight, trapped it between his front paws and began to gnaw.

Outside the cold store, Chef Billy Gordon, who got called either 'Flash' or 'Ramsey' depending on who he happened to be talking to, had just discovered a pool of yellow liquid on the floor of his immaculate kitchen.

He found it by stepping in it, the addition of liquid to the tile creating a near frictionless surface on which he slipped and almost fell. Staring at it with eyes agog, his mute horror flared and burned out like a safety match, replaced in an instant by incandescent rage.

That 'bleeper' of a sushi chef was at it again. Both men had been pranking each other for months, but Chef Kuroshio kept taking things too far. Billy suggested they should end the war before it got out of hand, and they shook on it. That was two days ago.

Now there was a pool of urine in his kitchen and there was too much of it to have come from anything other than a human. It wasn't as if one of the livestock animals could get up to the accommodation areas.

Taking a meat cleaver from a drawer, Chef Gordon stormed from his workspace, the earl's supper forgotten.

The cold store was sufficiently soundproof and airtight that Rex neither heard Chef Gordon's rant, nor smelled that he was there. He was too busy to be concerned by such trifling matters anyway; there was food to be eaten.

The kielbasa sausages went down a treat, so too the andouille. Several chunks from a range of German salamis were followed by a bite from the side of a whole parmesan cheese. Rex wasn't so keen on the parmesan, but the Shropshire Blue he found next possessed a delicate twang that went rather well with the Italian prosciutto.

It was all rather salty though. With his belly already filling and no intention of stopping, Rex concluded that what he needed was something to drink. It would cleanse his palate for a start. Equally, though, he hadn't taken a drink for a couple of hours and was getting thirsty.

He couldn't find anything though.

His nose knew there was no water present. Nor was there any milk, which would have been a happy substitute. In fact, Rex realised after a few minutes of searching, the only thing there was to drink, was whatever was in the rack of dark glass bottles arranged along one entire wall.

Bottles have liquid in them, but Rex's knowledge on the subject ended there. Presented with no options, he plucked one from the rack with his teeth, easing it out until the back end fell free. It broke the instant it made contact with the hard stone floor, the glass cracking so the deep red liquid inside spread across the floor.

Tentatively, Rex tried a little, dabbing his tongue where it had pooled under gravity away from the broken shards of glass.

Surprised to find it quite palatable, Rex lapped up all that he could before it drained away. Unsatisfied, he repeated the trick. The second bottle didn't break though. At least not straight away.

Rex tried a third and then a fourth. When none of them broke he decided he needed more height. Taking a bottle from a few feet up would do it. However, when he bounced up on his hind legs to grab one from above head height, he discovered the rack of bottles wasn't secured to the wall or the floor. It rocked back, startling the dog who jumped down just before it tipped.

The wine rack, one of many, didn't go far. It merely tipped to an angle of a few degrees. It probably would have recovered, but the bottles had other ideas. They began to slide from the holes in which they were resting, a cascade of vintage red wine leaping like lemmings to their ultimate doom.

Rex ran, his tail between his legs, using a centrally set table for cover as he peered out to watch the carnage. The smashing noise would have been heard by anyone in the kitchen, but the sound travelled no further than that through the dense layers of rock and soil from which the earl's lair had been carved.

When the ear-splitting sound of breaking glass subsided just a few seconds after it started, there was a small lake of red wine from which Rex slaked his thirst. Ready for seconds with an odd buzzing feeling in his head and a worrying yet somehow also joyous numbness throughout his body, Rex returned to the chilled meats.

Hoppy Hour

More than three hours after convincing a contingent of the pub's patrons to go with her to Thistle-Do-Me bed and breakfast at the top of the hill, Shelley led a ragtag band of seven mostly unwilling participants from the pub.

Each person had expressed a desire or interest in determining the truth behind the mysterious old vicar and were regretting their big mouths now. They might have been more willing were they not all quite so drunk.

Savvy enough to watch the tide of mood in his pub, the landlord had been swift to announce 'Hoppy Hour' just when it looked like people might begin to drift surreptitiously home. He'd never sold so much beer, so dropping the price for a couple of rounds made absolute sense. Especially when one discovers 'Hoppy Hour' only applied to the lagers and ales – the ones made from hops. The tactic ensured the blokes still paid full price for the ladies' drinks who were mostly drinking gin and tonic or white wine.

Seeing that Shelley was the instigator of the 'leave the pub' movement, he was sure to nudge a full glass of Guinness next to her almost empty one when she left her perch at the bar to visit the restroom. When she asked where it had come from, Glynn slyly indicated that Reg Postlethwaite had bought it. Reg was bald as a baby, seventy-three and wore a silk shirt with a large gold medallion nestling in his almost white chest hair. In the seventies, he was quite the catch and no power on earth would convince him anything had changed.

When Shelley looked his way, he winked, as Glynn knew he would, and the lie was sold. It meant she was staying for at least half an hour, which allowed the landlord time to get his wife out taking food orders.

"But we haven't got any food to serve, Glynn," Sally pointed out.

That wasn't going to stop him. Raiding his own freezer for everything he could find, sausages, burgers, or fish fingers all served with chips were on makeshift menu cards in an instant. Five minutes later they had forty-seven orders from the increasingly inebriated and hungry villagers which he delayed even starting to cook until everyone had bought at least one more drink.

Thus, three hours after she intended to set off on her quest to quiz Reverend Roy Hope about his reasons for visiting their tiny village and to settle several arguments about the winning betting slip, Shelley finally got her feet pointing in the right direction.

Curtis was with her, though he was flagging before they were halfway up the hill leading out of Glan-Y-Wern. The betting shop manager was more invested in finding the old man than anyone else. The call from Grand's PR department came less than an hour ago, forcing him to step outside where he could at least hear the voice at the other end.

It was here that the mystery deepened.

The vicar went by the name Roy Hope. The original bet was placed in Melton Mowbray by a man called Albert Smith. That was the name on the debit card.

The PR person, a lady with a posh London accent called Marissa Cardheart, warned Curtis there was something not entirely kosher about the vicar and his claim to the prize money. Curtis couldn't decide whether to feel relieved or disappointed. He'd been looking forward to a boost in business and takings, but at the same time worried about the inevitable slump that would follow. Whenever he managed to increase earnings in the past, head office was never impressed; they just wanted you to do the same again only bigger.

Miss Cardheart made it abundantly clear Curtis was to locate the winner and await further instruction. When he pressed to know more, she told him to make sure his shop looked like it had been opened yesterday. If there was a press event, there could not be weeds or litter in the gutter outside, there couldn't be smears on the windows and his staff had better get haircuts.

There was something she wasn't saying though. He could hear it in her tone – she was guarded. They knew something about the man – Albert Smith or Roy Hope, whichever it was, and Curtis knew if they could find a way to avoid paying, they would do so.

Ian Peck bounced out of an alleyway, startling Curtis and breaking his train of thought.

"Sorry, old boy," Ian slapped Curtis on the arm before zeroing his eyes on the street ahead and squinting because he believed it made him look dangerous. "Even the tip of the spear can't hold that much beer forever."

He left Curtis behind, ducking to edge around a car as if doing so might make him invisible. There were six other people meandering up the hill in plain sight. Quite what Ian thought he was going to achieve with his strange behaviour Curtis had no idea.

He did, however, need to pee now that Ian had raised the subject. Ducking into the mouth of the alley himself, he let the others get further ahead while he tended to a pressing need.

At the front of the rabble, if one ignored Ian which everyone was happily doing, Shelley puffed and plodded and wished the old man had been staying with Agnes. She was two minutes from the pub and on the flat.

Quite why Malory and Joshua had refused to answer their phones or respond to a single text message was beyond her, but given the additional information now in their possession – that Reverend Roy Hope had been in the possession of a betting receipt that was not his, it belonged to some poor chap called Albert Smith, her concern that something might have befallen the Hunt's, was genuine.

They arrived to find the B&B shrouded in darkness. There were no lights on inside and no sign that there might be anyone home.

The group of villagers knocked and called out, ringing the doorbell and tapping on the windows for fully five minutes before giving up.

Quitting their quest before achieving ... anything, came about not due to Shelley's own bladder which had processed five pints of stout and was fit to burst - she knew she wouldn't make it home and had hoped to use Malory's toilet had she been there - it was the arrival of a band of rain that saw to the intrepid investigators exploits that evening.

No one thought breaking in to check Malory and Joshua were okay was justified, and they were all thinking a nice night cap followed by a relatively early night was in order. Only Curtis hesitated when the rain started to come at them sideways. He was the one with a problem to solve. More than that, he was the least drunk. Or most sober, depending on which way you like to look at things, and had been the one to hear Marissa Cardheart's voice when she carefully didn't tell him what was going on.

The biggest single bet-winner in the firm's history might or might not be the man he met. Reverend Roy Hope held the winning ticket, but had he stolen it? Had he killed Albert Smith to obtain it? It would explain why he went to the most remote shop in the entire chain to cash it in and why he left the moment Curtis said he needed to check it.

Frustrated and getting soaked, Curtis checked down the hill. The rest of the party were running for cover. All except Shelley who obscurely appeared to be taking shelter under a low tree in the patch of scrubland down the road. He could see the streetlight reflecting on her face. Was she squatting?

He chose not to put too much thought to her choice of activity and went the long way to get back to his house.

In so doing he narrowly missed the very man he wanted to talk to.

Chilled to the Bone

Albert had a tear in his eye on his way back to the village. Fruitlessly he'd searched for Rex, shouting his name over and over until he became hoarse, and stumbling blindly in the dark to cover as much ground as possible. Though he desperately wanted to find his dog, fear that Rex wasn't answering because he was dead or mortally wounded filled Albert's mind and made him glad each time he explored a spot and found it devoid of his canine companion.

There was a steel rod in Albert's brain that refused to ever quit looking until Rex was found, yet he knew the reality of his situation.

Twenty years ago, he could take the punishment. Forty years ago he could have stopped to do some press ups along the way. Today, he knew that if he didn't head back to the bed and breakfast soon, he would succumb to the cold that had long since penetrated his layers of clothing. His legs were sore; his knees, hips and ankles protested their woe in that order of priority. He could no longer feel his hands nor anything below his wrists. His walk could best be described as a stagger so when the rain began to fall, he was already on his way back to civilisation.

Feeling sorry for himself was not in his nature, but if ever he were to do it, now was the appropriate time: Albert's spirit was about as low as it could possibly get.

The positive side of his mind knew his dog was young and strong and better able to withstand the climate than a human – Rex would be fine outside for the night. The argument was that Rex had vanished into thin air somehow. Wherever his dog was, Albert was certain he couldn't get to him until daylight now.

It was hard to accept, but Albert knew he was at the end of the road. Today his emotions had bounced up and down, reaching highs and lows as he thought he might be busted, to then believing he was on the right track and mere moments away from discovering where the elusive Gastrothief was hiding.

It was one thing to run the gamut of exhausting emotions with Rex safely at his side. Another proposition entirely to do it knowing his quest to bring one man to justice resulted in his dog being lost in the Welsh countryside.

If Rex was hurt or worse, Albert would never forgive himself and it was for that reason he now chose to give himself up. If he surrendered, there would be people willing to help find Rex. He wasn't going to phone the police; they would swarm him if he did. No, he would quietly contact one of his children, Selina perhaps. She would arrange his arrest in a manner that worked for Albert and see to it that Rex was found.

A grim smile played across his face even as his lips shivered and chattered from the cold – if he got lucky, they might trip over the Gastrothief while they were looking for Rex. It wasn't beyond the realms of possibility.

Sure, Albert had walked what felt like twenty miles back and forth between the main road and the tiny coast road without finding anything, but the gravadlax van had been going somewhere.

Feeling half frozen and unable to convince his fingers to work properly, it took more than a minute to open the front door of the B&B. He knew the Hunt's were out, the landlady had been good enough to warn him earlier. Plunging gratefully into the warmth of the house, he spared a moment to hope the couple were enjoying their anniversary.

Albert shared many with Petunia. Not enough, he mused sadly, but then what number could ever have satisfied him?

His coat and trousers were soaked. His boots too, the sturdy pair he favoured when he knew there was some walking to do. Staggering to his bedroom, the stairs presenting a fresh challenge to his frozen legs, he stripped his outer layer to discover what lay beneath was little better.

He was on his way home when the rain started, and had only to endure five or six minutes of it. However, the clouds coming in off the Atlantic and climbing to avoid crashing into the Welsh hills, chose to lighten their load in spectacular fashion. Big, fat, wet globules of rain worked through his parka in no time. It might once have been waterproof, but that was probably in the eighties.

His shirt joined the trousers on the radiator next to the socks. There wasn't room for his vest, but Albert figured he could rotate them later when the thinner items had dried.

In just his pants and still shivering for his skin was damp and the cold had wormed into his core, Albert shuffled to the connected bathroom where he used the wall for support when he turned on the bath's hot tap.

By the time steam billowed, he had a bath towel wrapped around his body, taken from a rather snazzy towel warmer so it imparted heat directly and immediately into his skin. In the bedroom again, Albert added the duvet, gripping one edge and rolling so it enshrouded his whole body. He couldn't stay that way for long; the water was filling his bath fast and he knew he would need to add cold soon, however stuck like that in the still and quiet, for the time being at least, his thoughts returned to Rex.

Food Coma

R ex was asleep.

The dog had a belly that on a female would be assumed to be filled with puppies. It could be recorded that he had eaten his fill, but such a simple phrase fails to capture the feast on which the German Shepherd had elected to gorge.

Several times, a small voice in his hindbrain raised a timid hand to suggest he might want to slow down or take a break. Stop perhaps? Rex didn't necessarily choose to ignore the voice, he just couldn't hear it over all the excited shouting coming from the rest of his brain.

Also, he would have told it to shut up and mind its own business had it managed to penetrate his consciousness.

Supremely satiated, there was little in the cold room that had gone unnibbled. It was all so good. So many flavours, almost all of which were too delicate for the dog's palate to understand. His nose might be among the most efficient on the planet, but his tongue was designed for licking mud from his coat – efficient and effective, but a blunt instrument rather than a finely tuned piece of machinery.

The food coma that followed his feast was as inevitable as it was unavoidable. For the best too, he knew when he laid his head down.

That he was trapped inside the room was a problem for later. There was a handle on this side, but he couldn't hope to operate it so he slept, hoping the disturbing sounds coming from his belly would subside before he woke.

It was cool in the room, but not so cold that it was going to stop him from sleeping.

Someone would come along sooner or later, Rex expected. Until then, his paws twitched in time to a dream about being chased by a veterinary nurse with a thermometer the size of a baseball bat.

Sending up the Distress Flare

Albert put so much cold water into his bath to make it bearable that it would have been considered lukewarm to anyone else. Submerging as much skin as he could, Albert gradually added more from the hot tap each time the water began to feel cool.

Over the course of nearly an hour, he brought his core temperature back from the dangerous level it had reached. Albert knew well enough that he'd been risking his life staying out as long as he had. Much longer and he might have become a statistic.

His stomach rumbled, signalling that it was time to get out. He was warm again, though his skin made goosebumps the instant he left the bath. Dinner ought to have been hours ago and he'd hoped to find something tasty at the pub by the harbour. It wasn't the only place to get food in the village, but the other venue was the chip shop and he'd already been there today.

Going out again was not an option, but he felt certain the Hunt's wouldn't begrudge him a couple of slices of bread from their kitchen.

First though, he needed to send the message to Selina. He'd been thinking about it and arguing with himself for more than an hour. The argument wasn't based on whether he should accept defeat or not; to resist now was tantamount to wagering Rex's life. The delay and internal discussion centred entirely on what to say and the fact that he couldn't figure out how to start and what to include.

The police were monitoring his children's phones and other communications devices, plus those of the people close to them. His friends too, so calling his neighbour, Roy Hope, was out of the question.

So how to get a message to them? He wanted someone he trusted to arrive first. Any of his children would fit the bill. The police would follow, and that was okay, but if he messed up and sent a message directly to anyone the authorities were watching, the local police would be on him in minutes.

To give himself time to chew over the problem, Albert went in search of toast and a cup of tea. He found both in the kitchen along with milk in the fridge and butter in a dish next to the microwave.

He did not hold back on the butter.

Feeling better now that he had something in his belly and further warmed by the hot drink, he returned to his room and took out his phone. His real phone, not the cheap one from the supermarket.

In his day there were no mobile phones. It was in the twilight of his career when the technology first began to appear on the streets. Even then, it was years before they became commonplace and many more after that when poorly funded organisations such as the police obtained the technology to track people using them.

Albert knew they could do it though. There would be a background program inside a computer somewhere that would ping the moment he turned it on. It was unavoidable, but he was going to turn it on, send a message and turn it off again. With the chip out – a task he'd needed a person in their twenties to perform for him, the signal would die.

The momentary blip would cause a reaction, but Albert hoped no more than that. They would be curious enough to send someone – how could they not? For all Albert knew, his phone showing up, even if only for a few seconds, might be the best lead they'd had in a week.

But the investigation was all the way across the country in London. Well, mostly. Plus, that annoying oik in Kent, Chief Inspector Quinn. Albert knew plenty like him. They came and went throughout his career. Quinn could smell an opportunity to further himself, a headline making collar that he could carry all the way to Chief Constable and beyond.

Quinn wouldn't know about the phone though, not unless he was really well connected. Which was possible, but even if he was, Albert couldn't see the man dropping everything and driving across the country, eight hours or more, just on a tiny hint of a lead.

The investigating team in London would get someone local to visit Glan-Y-Wern. A pair of constables probably. In a squad car, bored and uninspired by the task they'd been given.

That was best case scenario and moot really provided Selina or Gary or Randall got to him first. Boxed in by the inability to message them directly because that would tip the police off and send them running, Albert's fatigued brain finally hit upon a new idea: he could message someone to message his kids.

It was simple.

It was genius.

He wasn't entirely sure how to do it.

The list of contacts in his phone wasn't exactly long and extensive. In fact, when one removed his children and other relatives, of which there were very few, he had a couple of local contacts back home such as his neighbour, Wing Commander Roy Hope, and then there were the people he'd met on his tour around Britain.

Messaging Roy was out; the police were probably watching him just as closely as his children. It left the people he'd met in the last few months of travelling. Admittedly, he didn't really know any of them. The time he'd spent with any one of them could be measured in days on one hand.

A bond had formed though, or so he allowed himself to believe. Pass a message, that was a simple request, nothing onerous about it, right?

But who should he pick. In Melton Mowbray he met Donna Agnew. A lovely lass, but still a minor, so hardly the first person he ought to turn to in a crisis. The same could be

STEVE HIGGS

said of Asim and his cousin Afshin who he became acquainted with in Bakewell. They were technically adults and well trained martial artists to boot – hardly a factor in passing a message – but it was also fair to say they were over excitable and easily distracted. Albert went through a mental checklist of the other people he'd met.

In Stilton his companion was a young police officer called Oxford Shaw. He was a good lad, someone Albert could trust, but it would be unfair to ask the man to compromise himself by aiding a man he was duty bound to arrest. In Biggleswade he met Kate and Victor Harris. They were proper, dependable adults. He had a number for Victor somewhere in his phone. In Keswick he met Jaqueline ... Albert's face scrunched with effort, his brain refusing to supply the woman's last name.

Perhaps she never told him, Albert questioned. She had a German Shepherd too, a nice, calm, older lady dog called Maggie. She'd kept Rex in his place. The memory brought a smile to Albert's face, followed swiftly by a frown of worry.

Jaqueline was the ideal person to message. She was mature and sensible, and he wasn't asking much he reminded himself. There were a few others he could think of who he could ask for help with reason to believe they would give it. Gloria was one of them, but the eighty-something retired special ops undercover police officer was a little too nutso to be entrusted with a such a task. Not because she wouldn't do it, but because she would turn up in person driving a tank or something. Also, her pet snake, Chuckles, freaked him out.

No, Jaqueline was the right choice. In his head he composed what he wanted to write, inserted the chip into the little holder using a paperclip as the helpful 'young' person showed him and turned it on.

With next to no knowledge of such devices, Albert's heart performed a few double taps when nothing happened. The screen on his phone remained blank and lifeless. He pressed the on button again, this time holding it to see if that made a difference.

Was his phone broken? That was an obstacle to success he'd not considered. What could he do about it? Could he put the chip into a different phone? Would that work? Or were his contacts in the phone itself and not the chip?

94

He had no idea.

When the emblem for the manufacturer suddenly appeared a few seconds later, a sense of relief washed over him with such intensity it made him feel faint. Only for a moment though; that was all he got. His phone screen leapt to life with beeps, bells, and whistles as message after message and hundreds of missed calls cycled through.

Albert knew he needed to be quick, but couldn't help staring at the screen. There were dozens of calls from each of his children and from Roy, all of whom ought to know his phone was off. The messages flashed by too fast for him to read though he did catch the word newspaper article more than once.

He didn't want to know and didn't have the time to read them anyway.

Tapping the message app, he sought Jaqueline's name in his list of contacts. It wasn't there. Stuck yet again, Albert scratched his head and cursed under his breath. Her name had been in the phone, no power on earth could convince him otherwise.

So why couldn't he find it? He couldn't find anyone else for that matter. Asim wasn't there. Constable Oxford Shaw didn't appear either. Holding the phone with both hands, he banged it into his forehead, acting as though he might knock loose a memory to reveal where his contacts might have gone.

To his amazement, it worked. Apple-Blossom, his youngest granddaughter, rearranged the contacts in his phone when he was last with her. She put them into a group. Albert found it instantly and sagging with relief once again, he found Jaqueline and crafted the message he wanted to send.

Task completed, he turned the phone off and removed the chip. The process was supposed to take just a few seconds, that was what Albert told himself before he started. It had taken more than two minutes.

His phone had been on for two minutes. Long enough to register as more than a blip. In the dark recesses of his mind where Albert kept emotions such as anxiety and stress locked away behind bars, images of helicopters loaded with SWAT teams swam to life. They were heading his way already, multiple teams aiming to converge on the bed and breakfast.

The vision of men with guns and sunglasses continued to build, Chief Inspector Quinn's face sneering at him, looking down to where Albert lay curled and defeated on the ground. To his left and right, Gary, Selina, and Randall were in cuffs for helping him and Rex ... where was Rex.

Albert's right hand struck the side of his face with a 'smack' sound.

"Snap out of it, Albert," he cursed himself. He wanted to be out looking for Rex. He wanted to be doing ... something. Forced to accept the limitations of his body, hampered by his situation and solitude, Albert knew the only sensible thing he could do right now was get some sleep. His dog was far better able to survive the conditions outside and if Albert knew his dog the way he thought he did, he was willing to bet Rex had found somewhere dry and warm to sleep.

Overindulged

R ex was dry, but not exactly warm. He was also sick. Or, more accurately, he had been sick.

In a corner of the cold store, a regurgitated mound of cured meats and cheese bound together with an abundance of red wine cooled and slumped. Rex was back by the door, lying flat on one side where he enjoyed the cool seeping through his fur from the stone floor below.

It wasn't so much the overindulgence that made his stomach reject its contents, but the addition of copious amounts of alcohol. The majority of the red wine was back on the floor, yet his body had absorbed and processed enough of it that the room refused to stop spinning even when he closed his eyes.

In that moment he felt quite miserable. All that wonderful food gone to waste and rather than feeling full for the first time in his life, he felt terrible. He would sleep it off, that was what he told himself. A few hours of peaceful shut eye and he would feel much better.

He opened one eye to check the Iberico ham was still there. When he had recovered, he would try it again. Just with less gusto.

Cannot Stay, Cannot Leave

Sleep refused to come for Albert. Laying in his guestroom's giant double bed, his brain simply wouldn't shut off. Mostly it was worry for Rex, a wasted emotion for there was nothing he could do about his dog's situation. Not at night with the rain hammering against the windows.

Also, he thought about the message he'd sent and how quickly Jaqueline might react. Would she reply to his message asking for clarification? His phone was off with the chip removed. If she got no reply would Jaqueline attempt to do what he asked anyway? What if she didn't? How would he know if he didn't turn his phone on again?

Assuming she followed his request and instructions to the letter, how long would it take his children to arrive? Would they all come? That wasn't necessary and he'd asked Jaqueline to pass that on. He also knew what his kids were like. All three burst into the pork pie factory in Melton Mowbray expecting to find their father in dire straits or worse.

Also, it was late evening when he sent the message; what if Jaqueline didn't read it until the morning? There were enough 'what-if's' to drive a person insane.

Consequently, Albert was still awake when he heard the Hunt's returning from their night out. A quick glance at his clock showed the time at just after eleven. Rolling over, Albert did his best to arrange his limbs into a comfortable position and tried yet again to get some sleep.

There was no chance though and this time it wasn't his brain keeping him awake with random thoughts to make him worry, but the sound of the couple talking on the landing outside his room.

"Do you think he's in there?" asked Joshua, his voice a whisper that contained too much volume.

He'd been drinking, Albert guessed, his wife conceding to the driving duties. That had never been how he and Petunia did it. They either both had a drink or neither did.

"How should I know?" Malory replied, her words curt and a little snippy. "And don't you even think about going in there to check."

Silence followed for a beat or two before Joshua chose to challenge his wife's ruling.

"But what about all the texts? What if he is ... you know ... an imposter or a thief or something?"

Albert's eyes were wide now, and his body tensed in case he needed to make a hasty exit. Had they figured out who he was? Had they called the police? Surely not. If they were worried enough to dial 999, they wouldn't have waited outside, nor made their way up to bed. He could already hear someone brushing their teeth.

It was Malory, Albert discovered a moment later when she spoke around a mouthful of toothpaste.

"The messages from Shelley Rankin? You're not seriously going to tell me you believe the rubbish she said, are you? You can bet your next pay check she spent the whole evening in the Old Seamaster. She doesn't get those rosy cheeks from being exposed to the sea air you know."

Joshua wasn't in the mood to be dissuaded.

"Yeah, but what about Curtis Jones? He's a decent chap. He asked us to let him know that we were okay and to tell him when we got home. Said he needs to talk to our tenant."

"I'm going to bed. It's our anniversary, Joshua. That might not mean much to you ..."

Malory's husband did his best to protest and was cut off when his wife continued speaking.

"I will be in the bedroom. I expect you there once you've cleaned your teeth. You have work to do so you'd better hope that fourth beer doesn't affect your … performance."

"But our tenant might be a criminal, darling? Doesn't that concern you?"

"Not as much as the thought of Curtis Jones showing up at my house at midnight, no. You've met our tenant, right? He's a lovely old man … a vicar to boot and if he is using a fake ID, he still paid us up front. That's hardly criminal behaviour, Josh. Also, just in case you are thinking of opening his door to sneak around while he's sleeping, remember that he has a giant German Shepherd dog that will most likely bite your todger off if you give him so much as half a reason."

"Yeah. Good point," Joshua conceded, letting his right hand drop back to his side.

Albert listened for five minutes, propped up on one elbow with a hand poised to rip back his covers if the need arose. The thin bar of light under his door went out four minutes ago, but it wasn't until he could hear a trace sound of soft moaning that he dared to get out of bed.

The Hunt's were occupied for now, and Albert believed they wouldn't disturb him until the morning, but held no doubt they would have a few questions to ask when he appeared for breakfast. Curtis was the man from the betting shop, Albert remembered his name badge. That didn't mean they were talking about the same Curtis, but Albert dismissed the coincidence as unlikely. Shelley was the woman from the harbour and they both had cause to question the validity of his cover story.

Was that because they recognised him? His face had been all over the TV a week ago; maybe it still was. Whatever the case, he couldn't stay where he was. Not for long.

At the radiator, he discovered his trousers were still soaked. The radiator was cold, the heating having cycled off as one might expect. When had that happened? Albert guessed it must have been mere minutes after he draped his wet clothes over it. His coat, shirt and boots were no better.

He had another pair of shoes; loafers that were not exactly designed for cross country expeditions, but were functional, nevertheless. His small blue suitcase held spare trousers and shirts too, but the coat was a problem. It was the only one he had.

Pulling back the curtain just a touch to look outside, Albert saw the rain washing down the street outside in sheets. It was cold and wet outside and sunrise wasn't for many hours. Leaving now was foolhardy to say the least.

Puffing out his cheeks, Albert mulled over his limited options. Getting back into bed felt like an ostrich sticking its head in the sand. Regardless, it was the best choice available. If he could get a little sleep, he would be able to operate all the better tomorrow when he truly hoped to be answering questions and removing the monkey from his back. It wouldn't all go according to plan, how could it when there wasn't a plan? However, one way or another, Albert believed his remaining time on the run could now be measured in hours.

With an alarm set to wake him at five, Albert was going to leave the house before the landlord and landlady were awake. He could pinch some bread and marmalade to make a sandwich and be back searching for Rex and the Gastrothief's lair before the village of Glan-Y-Wern opened their eyes.

Quinn

More than two hundred miles east of Albert's location, Chief Inspector Quinn was also not sleeping. He had been, but the phone woke him.

"Where?"

"A tiny coastal village in Wales called Glan-Y-Wern. It's the absolute middle of nowhere," replied Sergeant Ulman with a quick check over his shoulder to make sure he was alone. He hated that he owed a debt to Chief Inspector Quinn. He hated to be in anyone's debt, but with Quinn you knew he was going to call it in at some point and not when it was convenient.

"Wales." Quinn remarked to himself. God, he hated the Welsh. They all talked so strangely, as if they deliberately chose to torture the English language with their accents. Wiping the sleep from his eyes, he swung his legs around and out of bed. "How recent?"

"A little more than an hour ago, Sir."

"An hour ago? And you're telling me now?"

Sergeant Ulman checked over his shoulder again.

"I shouldn't be telling you at all, Chief Inspector. There are detectives here working this case. If they find out ..."

"Then you'll be in the same compromised position that resulted in you needing to make this call, wouldn't you say?"

Ulman bit his lip at the barb.

"Who else knows?"

Ulman's brow furrowed deeply.

"You told me I had to squash the information if I could. No one else knows. The phone was only live for two minutes and thirteen seconds. I've already blanked the file the computer made so no one will ever know. We're square now, right?"

Quinn chuckled, "Goodness, no, Sergeant Ulman. You're eternally in my debt for not reporting your indiscretions. Now I want a better location than just 'a tiny village in Wales'. Get me an address and be sharp about it."

Squinting with confusion, Ulman asked, "You're going there, yourself?" He got no reply for Chief Inspector Quinn had already hung up.

On his bedroom floor, Ian Quinn performed fifty push ups in a single set and followed it with fifty sit ups – his daily routine whenever he got out of bed regardless of the time or who he was with. Bouncing back to his feet, he ran through a mental checklist of what he might need.

A packed bag waited in his utility room, the clothes inside neatly folded more than a week ago when he lost Albert Smith in Eton. In his head, Ian Quinn thought of himself as a hero to the people. He was tenacious and unstoppable. Whoever his quarry was. Wherever they might run. He would catch them.

Wales was far outside of his operating base, but the right to arrest people went with a police officer wherever they chose to roam. He had unused holiday time and fortuitously was off duty for the next two days anyway.

It was close to midnight but that just meant the roads would be empty. He could make it to Wales by breakfast easily. Maybe not all the way to the coast given how slow and winding the country roads were bound to be that far from civilisation, but he would be one of the first if not *the* first officer on scene.

All he had to do was catch Albert Smith. The story being run by The Independent Enquirer cast further doubt on the charges against Albert Smith and there were online and public campaigns to have the case dropped.

That wasn't going to happen, not without a full enquiry. Either way, he could arrest Albert Smith, something that would give him great pleasure, and if he was later proven to be innocent, Ian Quinn would claim to be the one who set out to ensure the old man was rescued and returned home with all charges dropped.

The point, he believed, with such a public case, was to be involved. His name had to be known. Repeated by reporters in television broadcasts and printed in the papers for all to hear and read and remember.

Albert Smith wasn't the full story though, and Ian Quinn clung to the hope that the boys in the Met were not focused on the daft Gastrothief story. Daft though it was, Quinn not only believed it might have an element of truth to it, he fervently hoped it did.

A true master criminal with a small empire of operatives stealing food and equipment, kidnapping people, and murdering. If it was true, then they were the people behind the explosion in Whitstable and all the charges against Albert Smith were false.

The article by Jessica Fletcher, all twenty-six pages of it, alluded to a mysterious figure one old man and his dog had been chasing all over the country. Quinn's own investigation suggested, if one was willing to suspend disbelief, that Albert Smith had been right all along. There was a strange sort of pattern to the crimes. Or they could just be random coincidences. Jessica Fletcher's story all but confirmed it.

Either way, Chief Inspector Ian Quinn intended to be the one in front of the cameras when the flashbulbs started popping.

Lifting a set of car keys from their hook by the door, he carried his ready-packed bag and a hastily constructed breakfast sandwich wrapped in tinfoil out through his front door.

THE GASTROTHIEF

He was going to Wales.

Unexpected Arrival

A lbert woke before his alarm, the human body demonstrating its ability to sense what was needed. Consequently, the alarm never rang, and the Hunt's didn't hear their guest sneaking quietly downstairs.

The sun was yet to make an appearance, but the sky outside was spectacular anyway. During the night the clouds were blown inland to reveal a star-filled sky and a bright, gibbous moon. Albert gazed in wonder for a moment, the spell breaking with a shiver when the cold air snuck down the back of his collar.

His parka coat was still damp and no good to wear. The radiators were cold to the touch when he tested them at five o'clock. It didn't come as a shock; his wouldn't be on either. It left him with jumpers and a jacket, plus a hat, gloves and scarf which he'd thankfully forgotten to wear the previous day.

Wrapped up as warm as he could be, with multiple layers to keep the cold air from his skin, Albert stepped out from the shadows by the front door of the B&B. There was no one around. Barely any sign of life at all until one turned toward the harbour.

Faint sounds drifted up from the small port and though he was too far away to make out people in the pre-dawn gloom, lights from the cabins and those shining over the decks created silhouettes and shadows where the fishermen moved.

One of his worst fears in the moments when worry nudged Albert from his slumber, was that he would awake to find police cars in the street outside. Tracking the road that led into the village as it swept up the hill and out of sight, there was no sense that a squad car was about to burst into sight at break-neck speed with its lights flashing.

Perhaps it meant they wouldn't come, and his calculated risk would pay off. Selina might appear later today. Or it could be one of his sons, Gary or Randall. If they were being clever, it would not be all three of them.

Of course, he was far from convinced his message had been received. Was Jaqueline even now snoozing in her bed oblivious to his plight?

Albert's right hand twitched, rising toward his jacket where both phones resided in an inside pocket. Should he turn the phone on and check? He'd made it through the night without the police storming the bed and breakfast.

Wavering in his indecision, Albert convinced his feet to start walking. His hips, knees, and lower back ached from the arduous hours spent searching for Rex the previous evening. A couple of good painkillers would take the edge off, but he didn't have any and there was nowhere he could go to obtain some. Not without trekking to the next village along the coast.

Telling himself his joints would ease once he was moving, he aimed for the main road. There he would turn right and head back to the general area where he last saw Rex. The sun would be up in an hour or so, the first tendrils of sunlight due to appear very soon.

With light as his ally, he would find Rex, and everything would be all right in the world.

However, just as he reached the intersection and could start the climb up the hill and out of Glan-Y-Wern, a distant sound made Albert turn through a hundred and eighty degrees. Initially, he thought the distant thrum of an engine accompanied by a thumping bass beat must have come from one of the fishing boats as it got ready to make sail.

It hadn't though, a fact that became obvious when he was facing the harbour. The sound, continuing to increase in volume, was coming from a car. Given how much noise it was making, one would be forgiven to assume it was baring down on Albert's location, but the offensive automobile was still on the road into the village.

It had to be at least a mile away.

Dismissing it, Albert turned away, pushing off with his right leg to get started on the steep hill.

He took only one pace before a little voice inside his head insisted he take another look at the car. Albert couldn't exactly see it in the dark, but there was something disturbingly familiar about it anyway.

Frowning now and staring at the quad headlight beams piecing the darkness, Albert bit his bottom lip and told himself it was just his imagination.

It had to be.

He kept watching though. Kept watching until the car reached the outskirts of the village and passed under a streetlamp. Waiting to get a better look at it and certain that would dispel his overactive imagination, Albert almost spat out his teeth when he saw the car's colour.

It was purple.

Sparkly purple.

It was a sparkly purple convertible Mercedes and how many of those could there be on the planet?

The music shut off, the air abruptly devoid of noise as the car slowed and the growl of its engine quietened to a hungry purr.

Albert couldn't see who was in the car, but he didn't need to – there could only be one person behind the wheel.

Confused, amazed, bewildered, and reeling from a host of other related emotions he didn't even have names for, Albert stepped into the road and lifted both arms. Waving them slowly up and down to attract the driver's attention, he saw when he was spotted. The car leapt forward again, the driver abandoning the stealthy approach to once again gun the engine.

Albert let his arms drop. What emotion was he supposed to feel at this point? Relief for certain.

The car belted up the hill, coming straight for him. Albert stepped out of the road and onto the grass verge where he waited until the driver slammed the brakes and the immensely modified car went from eighty miles per hour to nothing in a laws-of-physics-defying distance.

"Hey, Bruv!" bellowed Asim to be heard over the roar of his engine. "What's up, innit? You're a total badass these days."

"Geezer!" joined Afshin from the passenger's seat.

Albert leaned on the edge of the roof and bent from the waist to look inside the car.

"Hello, Asim. Afshin." He gave each man a nod and shook their hands when they reached across. "I must say it is lovely to see you both again, but I have to ask what you are doing here and how it is that you found me? I mean, you're not here by accident, I assume." Albert had already calculated the likelihood of two young men from Bakewell in Derbyshire finding their way to Glan-Y-Wern in Wales on a whim.

Nearest to Albert, Asim twisted in his seat to look at his cousin, Afshin. Albert couldn't see the expression on Asim's face but guessed it must be one of question because Afshin shrugged and made a 'beats me' face.

Asim's eyebrows were deeply set in curious mode when he turned around again.

"You asked us to come, Bruv. So we came."

Albert blinked and gave a small shake of his head.

"I'm sorry, I did what?"

Asim fished out his phone from a pocket in the front of his hoody.

"It's right here, Bruv." Asim fiddled with the screen, scrolling and then dabbing it to bring up the message he wanted. "Well, I guess you didn't exactly ask us to come, but you made it sound like you were in trouble and close to taking down the Gastrothief, Bruv."

Albert's brain registered confusion when Asim employed the term 'Gastrothief'. How did Asim know it? He met the young man way back in Bakewell, less than a week into his journey around the country. The concept of the Gastrothief didn't emerge until after he left Stilton.

Asim was still talking as he handed Albert his phone, "If there's going to be some major hero stuff going on, Afshin and me want to be in on it."

"Yeah," agreed Afshin, "the chicks dig a bit of hero stuff. Maybe we can, like, get our faces in the paper or something."

Increasingly bewildered, Albert read his own words.

'I hope you will excuse me for reaching out like this. I am in dire straits as I am sure you have seen on the news. Please believe that I am innocent of all charges the police suggest I might be guilty of. Just like the time I spent with you, I am engaged in trying to solve a crime, a serious one, but in my investigation I will admit to have taken some wrong turns.'

Albert tutted at how much he had rambled and continued to read.

'I reach out to you at this time because I fear I have reached the end of my journey. It is time to accept defeat and put an end to the wasted effort at the hands of the police. I will give myself up, but wish to do so on my own terms. I cannot contact my children directly – each of whom is a senior police detective – and ask that you do so for me. I hope that is not too much to ask.'

His message proceeded to list the name and addresses for his children – all three because he wanted to give Jaqueline options and increase her chance of success – and provide a message to pass on: 'I am in the Welsh coastal village of Glan-Y-Wern. The Gastrothief is here, but despite finding the yacht on which one of his agents escaped Cornwall, I have been unable to locate the Gastrothief's base of operations or even determine who he or she *is. It is time for me to surrender. Not because I am hurt or in trouble (anymore than you already know about) but because I have lost Rex. He vanished while we were searching for the Gastrothief's lair. Much as I want to emerge victorious from my quest, I cannot risk Rex's life to achieve my goal. If one of you can find me here and take me into custody, please do. If that proves beyond the scope of reality, please do whatever you can to assist my surrender. I await your arrival. Your loving father.'* His message ended with a heartfelt thank you to Jaqueline and his hope that both she and Maggie were in good health.

It was exactly as he remembered writing it. Yet it had gone to the wrong person. Frowning deeply, he pushed his brain to bring forth the image of his phone when he scrolled through the contacts to find Jaqueline. He would swear under oath he had sent it to her.

Handing the phone back to Asim, he said, "Well, I must start by thanking you for coming. You must have dropped everything to have made it here so quickly."

Asim nodded, stifling a yawn with the back of his left hand. When it subsided some seconds later, he nodded again.

"Pretty much, Bruv."

Leaning across the car's transmission tunnel, Afshin said, "After we'd contacted your kids first though, innit? We made sure to follow your advice."

Part of Albert's instruction had been to employ a motorcycle courier to deliver his message in a typed or handwritten format – he couldn't come up with another way to get around the police monitoring their communications devices. Phone, text, and email were out and posting a letter would take too long.

"Who's Maggie though, Bruv?" Afshin wanted to know. "We went through all the people we could remember meeting with you and don't recall a Maggie at all."

Asim asked, "Is she fit?" with a tone that suggested she could not have been for then he would most definitely have remembered her.

Albert's brain was still trying to figure out how he could have messaged Asim and not Jaqueline, but since the boys claimed to have messaged his children, he accepted that it didn't matter.

"You sent a motorcycle courier to find my children?" he tried to confirm.

"Yes, Bruv," Asim nodded around another yawn.

"Well, sort of," added Afshin. Sensing the old man was going to want some clarity on his statement, Asim's cousin said, "Here, is there anywhere around here to get some breakfast? We're starving."

"Yeah," agreed Asim, whipping out his phone. "We figured we would find a McDonald's or something along the way, but there hasn't been a building with its lights on for the last hundred miles."

Albert chuckled, "Sorry, boys, you'll not find a fast-food place around here. Not unless you count the chip shop and that won't be open for hours."

Staring in horror at his phone Asim exclaimed, "Bruv, the nearest Maccy Dees is forty-seven miles away. We're gonna starve!"

Afshin's jaw dropped.

Trying to stave off the rising panic, Albert ventured, "I have a couple of granola bars in my jacket. They've a little smooshed, but you can have them."

Asim didn't reply for a moment. Both he and his cousin were bent over Asim's phone, fiddling with the screen.

"There's a café in the next village. Says it opened at five and serves a full English breakfast," revealed Asim with a sigh of relief.

Afshin settled back into his chair. "Yeah, but I bet they do something weird and Welsh with it. Like maybe they serve leeks instead of bacon or something."

Albert doubted very much that would be true but could not provide a response based on experience.

Asim shuddered. "Well, we gonna find out soon enough, Bruv. You coming, Albert?"

"I need to look for Rex, chaps. Sorry."

Asim peered out into the dark morning air. "You need to start right now? It will be light in half an hour, Bruv."

Albert's mouth opened, a rejection forming on his lips. Asim was right though. It made sense to wait until the sun was up. Also, he'd eaten four pieces of bread in the last almost eighteen hours. He was hungry and the energy boost would do him good. Not only that, he needed to pick their brains – Afshin said they sort of employed a motorcycle courier. What did that mean exactly?

Breakfast Surprise

R ex's mouth was dry. He woke to a terrible thirst matched only by a thumping headache. The red wine he'd enjoyed the previous evening held no allure now, so he stayed thirsty and due to his parched mouth managed only to nibble on a few pieces of the ham. He was hungry, but not in the mood to eat.

Still trapped in the cold store, which had penetrated his fur coat and was beginning to cool his blood, he paced and paced around in a long circuit that took him past the ruined hams and sausages, through the destruction of cheeses, and skirted the wrecked wine racks.

Stuck where he was last night, Rex chose to make the best of it. Now he wanted out. Ten minutes of pawing at the door achieved nothing and sent him back to pacing.

Though Rex could not see it, the lights had just come on in the kitchen beyond the cold store's door – Chef Billy Gordon had arrived to begin making the earl's breakfast. His first breakfast to be more accurate because he always had more than one. In Earl Bacon's opinion breakfast was too good for a person of means to limit themselves to just one a day.

The first of the Arbroath Smokies, smoked in their underground biome where they were safe from the impending cataclysm above, arrived in his kitchen yesterday. Argyll, the man from Arbroath responsible for producing the Scottish delicacy, complained bitterly about not only his captivity – most of them complained about that – but also that the fish were all wrong for smoking. It wasn't the right fish, they weren't big enough, he wasn't being given the right wood ... They looked good enough to Billy and when he tasted them, they were sublime.

The earl was excited to try one himself, so when he was ready, Billy set out a plate and headed toward the cold store. Halfway there he stopped dead in his tracks.

A thin line of what was blatantly red wine was trickling out from under one edge of the door. From there it ran to a drain in the floor and vanished.

The colour drained from Billy's cheeks. The earl had three wine cellars, each set at a different temperature depending on the nature of the wine being stored and the advice given by their vintner, another person who complained they were being held captive when really they were being saved just like the earl said.

Praying he would find just one or two broken bottles and that the glass might have simply failed rather than he left something balanced precariously and it fell onto the wine – the earl was not known for his forgiving nature – Billy grabbed a mop and bucket from the corner of the kitchen.

With hot water and some cleaning fluid, he mopped up the trickle outside the door before anyone could happen to pass and see it. Then, with his heart in his mouth, he placed both hands on the door's push bar.

"What's he having for breakfast this morning?" asked Sabrina Ticehurst.

Billy squealed in fright and spun around, his eyes wide and his heart on strike. With one hand on his chest he tried to speak.

Sabrina giggled, "Sorry, did I startle you?"

She was there deliberately, dropping by to say hello on her way to the gym. The earl didn't approve of physical exercise, but didn't mind too much if other people were doing it. The gym had been added to his original plans for the biome when the people he recruited, rather than those he had kidnapped, said they wanted it.

Sabrina liked to keep fit and had intentions towards Billy. She'd been flirting with him for weeks; not that he was getting the message.

"Startle me? You damn near killed me."

She laughed a little harder. "I'm sure you'll be fine. I can make it up to you later though, if you like." She winked saucily.

Billy knew he was being flirted with, but liked his women with a bit more meat on their bones. Keen to get rid of her, he asked, "Was there something you wanted?"

Now frowning, Sabrina folded her arms across her chest and scowled. "No, I guess not."

"I won't keep you then."

Sabrina was about to fire a snarky retort about Billy's waistline, a feature she'd been willing to overlook given the tiny pool of available men to pick from, but the insult died in her mouth when she spotted something else.

"What's that, Billy? Is that … is that blood?"

Billy's eyes shot down, tracking where Sabrina was looking. The trickle of red wine was back, seeping out from under the edge of the door.

Looking back up, he found Sabrina's face had gone pale – she thought he'd killed someone and stashed the body.

"No, it's not what you think! It's just a little red wine. I think a bottle must have broken during the night."

Keeping her distance and certain she could outrun the burly chef if he came for her, Sabrina challenged, "Show me."

On the other side of the cold store door, Rex had heard Billy squeal in fright a few moments earlier and was poised to react if the door opened. With his legs tensed and his tail ramrod straight, he was ready to escape his temporary prison the second the door opened.

Thinking better of it, he darted across to the hams littering the floor, grabbed one and went back to his position facing the door. At least he had a snack now for when he'd managed to slake his thirst.

The sound of the push bar depressing teased at Rex's coiled spring stance. He jerked, almost leaping forward to get out but the door had to open inward.

A human's voice filled the air and Rex caught his scent. It was the same man he'd smelled in the kitchen yesterday.

"It's just some red wine. You'll see."

Billy's assurances ended abruptly when something hit his legs at speed. Flipped into the air, the terrified chef caught a glimpse of something tan, black, and furry moving beneath him at breakneck speed. It was little more than a blur and the air was filled with his yell of alarm plus a high-pitched scream from Sabrina.

Rex shot by the woman half blocking the kitchen's exit, turned right just as he had the previous day, and bolted along the corridor. There was no attempt at stealth this time around. With all the noise the humans were making, Rex believed his only available strategy was to vacate the area and that was what he intended to do.

Once again he could smell the sea. The tang of musty air, laced with damp earth and a million other scents impacted his olfactory system as he ran. He could use it to navigate, but only if he knew where anything was, which he didn't.

All he had was best guess and blind luck to find his way back to the surface. Yesterday, he'd wanted to track Tanya, his sense of justice dictating he attempt to apprehend her for her crimes. Today, though, he just wanted to get back to his human. It had been many hours since he fell through the hole in the ground, and he worried for the old man.

Albert had a habit of getting into trouble. Rex needed to reassure himself that his human was all right. Then he would figure out how to tell him about Tanya.

Catching a whiff of air that bore the same greasy smoke he encountered in Arbroath, Rex found a junction and followed it. Maybe he could find Argyll and he could help to get Rex back to daylight.

World Famous Detective

A t a table tucked into the corner of a small café on the seafront in Abergowd-Coed, Asim, Afshin, and Albert awaited their breakfasts with barely contained impatience. To kill time, the boys were explaining what they did when they got Albert's message.

"We got Malac to do it," Asim revealed.

"Malac?"

"Yea, Bruv, he's a wicked street racer. Why give work to a motorcycle courier when one of the crew has a motorbike?"

Afshin joined in, "Yeah, he's like a total radical Street Hawk for the 21st century, Bruv! He would have driven two hundred miles in like an hour and a half, innit."

Translating at speed, Albert sought confirmation, "So you asked a friend to deliver the messages?"

The boys nodded and replied in unison, "Yes."

"And you wrote down the message I sent for my children so it could be hand delivered?"

Again he got a response from both men as it they were operating with one brain.

"S'right."

"I guess that should do it. You're sure you can trust him?"

Asim was taking a slurp of tea so his cousin answered, "Yeah, Bruv, Malac's a geezer, but he wouldn't mess up on a secret mission."

Putting his cup down, Asim asked, "Anyway, Albs, what's going on with you? You're this fairy tale Robin Hood character now. The five-oh are after you, but the country is all up in arms to support you."

"I'm sorry, what?" Albert heard what was said, but didn't understand it.

Asim's reply was cut off by a loud shout coming from the café's front door.

"Albert!"

Three dozen heads turned to look at the young woman coming through it. Accompanied by a teenage boy roughly her age, she made a beeline for Albert's table.

Albert could scarcely believe his eyes.

"Donna?"

Afshin leaned in close to his cousin. "Who's the babe? Do you know her?"

Asim shrugged, flicking his gaze to Albert for enlightenment.

"Donna what are you doing here?" he looked away from her to the boy standing in her shadow. "And Toby." Albert recognised him too.

Donna's eyebrows did a little dance as she ran Albert's response through her head.

"You said you were in trouble, Albert. You said you were in trouble, that you were about to catch the Gastrothief, and that you had lost Rex. We got one of Toby's brothers to take the message to your kids in Kent, and drove straight here. Well, we went to Glan-Y-Wern, but there's nothing open there and this is the nearest place serving food."

"Yeah, we're starving," added Toby.

Donna had used the name 'Gastrothief'. She was the second person to do so in the last half an hour and it required comment.

"How do you know that name?" Albert asked.

Donna had to step back when a waitress appeared with three plates of breakfast.

"What name?"

Albert mumbled his thanks to the lady with the food, moving his arms from the tabletop and shifting his cutlery so she could put his plate down.

"Careful, the plates are hot," the waitress warned. "Is that everything?"

"Can I get the same?" asked Toby, taking a seat at an adjacent table. "You want anything, Donna?"

Donna rolled her eyes. "Always thinking with your stomach." To the waitress, she said, "Two of the breakfasts, please. Same as theirs, but no grilled tomato for me, thank you."

"I'll have hers," volunteered Toby, sounding hopeful for an extra ration.

Forcing his way into the conversation again, Albert said, "The Gastrothief. How do you know that name? Where did you hear it?"

Donna blinked, failing to give an answer while she looked at the two young men sitting opposite Albert. They bore the same surprised expression.

Sliding into the chair opposite Toby and directly across the gangway from Albert, Donna said, "Albert, everyone in the country knows that name."

Asim swallowed his mouthful of breakfast to agree. "She's right, Bruv. How do you not know that? Talk of the Gastrothief and your quest to find him is everywhere."

Feeling something akin to dizzy, Albert shook his head. It was like falling through the looking glass and he found himself asking, "What are you talking about?"

121

All four of his young companions were on their phones already. Donna was the first to turn hers so Albert could see.

There, in the centre of the screen was a picture of Albert Smith. Not as he is now, but one of him in his best dress uniform not long before he retired.

"The story broke a few days ago," Donna explained.

"It was Thursday," Toby chose to be exact. He shut up when Donna shot him a look.

Asim argued, "Well, my main man, Albert here, has been in the news for weeks. That was when they were trying to convince everyone he was like a terrorist or something, though."

"Yeah," chipped in Afshin, "but we both said there's no way, man. Albert's a total geezer. If there's explosions and stuff happening, it's because he's getting too close to cracking someone's drug ring."

"Yeah, or human trafficking," said Asim.

"Except it's someone kidnapping chefs and stealing food," remarked Donna, her eyes locked on Albert's as his skipped across the screen of her phone.

Reading the first lines of the article with utter disbelief, Albert's head swam in a sea of gloopy confusion. The name at the top was Jessica Fletcher, the woman he met in Eton. He knew she was an investigative reporter, and he recalled spilling his guts on the long drive from Berkshire to Cornwall. He'd told her everything he knew and regaled her with reconstructions of the events in each of the towns he and Rex had visited on their travels.

Jessica had turned it into a story. One that countered the previous news story where he was a wanted man and potentially a terrorist.

His lips numb, Albert mumbled, "You say everyone knows about this?"

Donna did nothing to hide the shock she felt. Albert genuinely had no idea how famous he was. Reaching across the gap between their tables, she placed a hand on his forearm.

"Albert, this is a huge social media event."

"Yeah, Bruv," Afshin talked around the mouthful of food he was chewing. "It's not just here either. This is global, Bruv."

Donna continued, "Everyone wants the police to drop the charges against you and investigate the Gastrothief. Your son, Gary ..."

Albert's ears pricked up.

"He was on the ten o'clock news two days ago and on the BBC breakfast show the day before that. He told them he's been suspended from his job pending a full enquiry and might be dismissed from the Metropolitan Police for attempting to help you."

Albert winced to hear the news.

The waitress returned with two more breakfast plates. She delivered them both but instead of retreating as one might expect, she paused, her gaze aimed at Albert.

"Here, are you that fella from the TV?" she wanted to know. "The one with the dog who's trying to catch the Gastrothief?"

Albert's instant instinct was to deny he had any idea what she was talking about, but he didn't get the chance.

Asim got in first. "That's right, sugar. This here is Albert Smith. The most famous detective in the whole world."

Looking pleased with herself, the waitress produced her phone from a back pocket.

"Ooh, I'll have to get a selfie."

Before Albert could move, the woman had turned, crouched and grabbed a snap with her face next to Albert's.

Returning to upright, she said, "What are you doing here in Wales then? If you don't mind me asking."

Yet again, Albert got no chance to answer for himself.

This time it was Toby who jumped in. "This is where the Gastrothief's secret lair is hidden," he replied, far too loudly for Albert's liking.

The waitress laughed. "What? Here? I don't think so, kid. Nothing ever happens here."

She chortled as she wandered back to the counter at the back of the shop to tell her colleagues who they had as a visitor.

Still reeling from the revelations of the last few minutes, Albert stuck his fork into a piece of sausage.

"I need to go. Rex is still out there somewhere and if you both delivered the message to my children, then you can bet there's a whole truckload of police going to be heading this way very soon. Social media following or not, I still have some very difficult questions to answer. It will be a whole lot easier for me if I have found where the Gastrothief is hiding." Albert's sausage was heading for his mouth when his fork stopped moving. "Hold on. How did both of you get my message? I only sent it to one contact."

The question hung in the air for a moment, all five people looking at each other in question.

Across the café, two men stepped away from their table. Sharing a silent glance they both understood, they left the eatery and walked out of sight.

Honour First

Parked outside the Old Seamaster, Constable Oxford Shaw stepped out of his car and zipped his coat all the way up under his chin to keep the cold out.

In the harbour, fishing boats were chugging out to sea, their running lights making those further away easy to spot. The sun was just peeking over the horizon, a deep orange ball of burning gas bringing light to the Welsh coastline. It was probably bringing warmth too, but shivering in the cold air, Oxford couldn't feel it.

Receiving Albert's message the previous evening, he found himself furiously debating what he ought to do. The right thing, from a career perspective and as a police officer, was to immediately notify his superiors and let them handle it.

However, not only had he been interviewed by Jessica Fletcher for the article published in The Independent Enquirer, he knew Albert Smith personally and that set him apart from almost everyone else on the planet. In Oxford's eyes, Albert Smith was an honourable man, and no one would convince him otherwise.

The allegations of terrorism shocked him when he first saw the news reports. He remembered sending Albert a message at the time and trying to call him. The text messages were never answered, and the calls met with a dead signal every time.

It happened again last night when out of the blue a lengthy message popped into his phone. That it came from Albert was a jolt, especially when he read it. Oxford tried calling only to receive the same dead signal he always got. He knew what it meant: Albert had removed the chip from his phone and switched it off. It was a wise tactic if he didn't want to get caught, but given the upwelling of public support, surely Albert would benefit from revealing where he was.

In the message Albert claimed to be close to the Gastrothief's lair. Oxford attempted to recall his exact words ... Albert said he knew he was in the right place, but couldn't find it. Something like that.

Oxford would have come running the moment he knew where Albert was and no matter what he wanted. Albert chose to help when he had no reason to and saved Oxford's life while risking his own. However, there was a thing Oxford remembered among all the lessons he learned during his few short days in Albert's company: arresting people and taking them into custody was the sole remit of the police. Albert might find the criminal in any given investigation, but he needed a police officer to apprehend the suspect.

Oxford came to Wales to do just that.

Using his own money, he sent a motorcycle dispatcher to the addresses Albert gave for his children, then got in his car and started driving. He was abandoning his post and would be reprimanded for it, but there were more important things in life than career. Honour for a start.

He was here because it was the honourable thing to do.

The village was waking up to a new day; a jogger ran past on the other side of the street, and to Oxford's left, a woman in her sixties emerged from her front door to walk her dog.

There was no traffic around which was why he noticed the sound of approaching vehicles. It stood out in the quiet of the coastal village where he could hear every wave lap against the shore. Two large cars were heading for Glan-Y-Wern; Range Rovers, Oxford thought though it was hard to be sure in the still dim light of early dawn. His guess was based on the shape of their headlights. They were tailed by a large silver van. A ford Transit, he guessed.

Dismissing them as insignificant, Oxford crossed the road, fetching up against the sea wall, there to keep the tide at bay if it ever chose to reach inland. He'd come this far, but what now? The task at hand was to find Albert and assist him. It was a small village, but even so, there had to be a thousand houses, a few thousand residents. Spotting a woman with ruddy cheeks crossing the harbour with a thermos flask tucked under one arm, he vaulted over the wall.

He would start with her and keep asking until he found someone who had met or seen Albert. Someone would know where he was staying.

The Cold Store

The cold store was a wreck. The contents were ruined. It wasn't just that the dog had smashed a collection of rare wines which Chef Billy already knew could never be replaced, it was the meats and cheeses from around the world too. And more because not only had the dog clearly eaten so much he'd vomited – there was a disgusting pile of partially digested food in one corner – the dog had also needed to use the facilities during his incarceration, so there was a pile of an altogether different nature right underneath the first batch of Arbroath Smokies.

It was still steaming.

No one was ever going to want to eat anything from the cold store ever again.

Sabrina hadn't offered to help Billy when the dog bounded straight through his legs, felling him in an instant. Instead, she ran away screaming like she was on fire. Any chance he had of covering up the destruction or salvaging enough of the hams and cheeses that the earl might not notice went up in smoke when the first people arrived less than twenty seconds later.

The second person through the door was one of the earl's muscular cretins; the ones he sent out to get the things and the people he wanted. They gave Billy the creeps. Especially Tanya. She was an attractive woman, but the kind who might stab you if you bought her the wrong kind of flowers.

Thankfully, it wasn't Tanya today, it was Ladd, but he wasn't a whole lot better.

"He's on his way," Ladd chose to share.

"The Earl?" Billy blurted, startled and horrified by the news. Feeling that he was about to be blamed, Billy chose to point out, "It wasn't my fault. I didn't put the dog in there."

A laugh split Ladd's face. "What then? The dog let himself in? Well known for opening doors dogs are." He was sharing a joke with Evan, an equally dangerous looking individual and another of the earl's hired killers.

Chef Billy looked away, his gaze falling on the destruction inside the cold store once again. He closed his eyes, wondering if today might be his last.

"I, um ... I need to visit the gents," he announced, thinking he might slip away and exit the underground biome before the earl could flip out and have him killed.

Ladd lifted one muscular arm, his palm out. His shoulders filled the doorway where he blocked Chef Billy's exit from the kitchen.

"The earl will be along soon. You can hold it until then." It was an order, not a question. "You know," Ladd sneered, "I had to go all the way to Spain for that ham."

Chef Billy didn't know who had collected what; there was so much food, who could ever keep track of it? That Ladd was the one who collected the ruined Iberico ham went some way to explain his attitude.

In the distance, the sound of the earl's unhappy, disbelieving, and rage-filled tone echoed against the rock.

Chef Billy looked at the knives on his counter and tried to calculate his chances.

The Biome

B ounding through the maze of underground passages, Rex's nose caught a whiff of Tanya at one point, yet he chose to ignore it: there was a longer strategy in play. His nose also found Kelly, the other woman from Cornwall. She was easier to dismiss – she hadn't shot Rex in the bum with electricity or tried to blow him up.

It took more than ten minutes for Rex to find his way out of the earl's accommodation area, following his nose toward the smells he believed would lead him to people. Friendly people.

Finally reaching a door, he was defeated by a locking mechanism that was not operated by pressure on a push bar. Mercifully, the handle wasn't a knob, so although it took umpteen attempts and hurt his teeth, he managed to drag the lever downward through a sufficient arc to open the door. Then he had to back away as it opened inward. His head was canted to an awkward angle, but Rex was not in a mood to let a silly human barrier beat him.

What Rex did not know was that the door only opened from the inside. The security team working for the earl were habitual in keeping the doors shut. A sniff of freedom might convince the residents living in the livestock and farming areas of the biome that rising up against their captors was a worthwhile endeavour.

It wasn't. The security team was armed, and most were ex-military. They would shoot and kill if necessary, but that would deplete the number of people making food to support those living in the biome. Better to give the residents no hope.

It was light beyond the door. Rex had put no thought to what time of day it was. It felt like breakfast time, and he was hungry. His thirst and headache continued to dictate he find water before attempting to eat anything, so when his ears detected the babbling sound of a river, he pointed his nose toward it.

Loping along at an easy pace, Rex's canine brain paid no attention to the magnitude of the cavern he now found himself in. Huge lights stationed high above his head shone down to fill the underground cave with light. There were farm animals here, their smell hanging thick in the air. Pigs, cows, sheep, chickens, and more. With the smells stuck inside the cave, Rex struggled to pinpoint where each came from, but his eyes provided the answers.

Sprawling across the ground were fields in which crops grew. There were polytunnels – not that Rex knew the name for them – in which many different crops were grown. In many ways it was testament to the Earl's insane genius that the people growing the crops had to do so, in order that they themselves would survive.

The underground biome had to be self-sufficient. Either they all lived or none of them did. Once the outer doors were shut for good, there would be no escape.

Of course, there was another way to get out. It was the original way into the cavern, but so far as Earl Bacon knew, he was the only one who knew of its existence and how to reach it.

Rex found the water, a fresh stream of it. It was filtering down through the rocks above, multiple little streams gathering to make a babbling brook that then flowed into a fresh-water lake.

Rex drank, savouring the refreshing chill of the cold water. Taking a breather so he could eat, Rex idly tore off a chunk of ham. Gnawing at the bone trapped between his front paws, the German Shepherd looked down at the scene below. He was twenty feet above the fields, still among the craggy rocks on which nothing could be grown.

Pens containing the various animals – enough to support a small community – kept them in place. Humans were moving about, going through the routine of their daily activities. A cry pulled Rex's head to the left where he saw two children, one chasing the other in a game.

With something in his belly and his thirst in the background finally, he abandoned the rest of the ham, got to his feet, and set off: it was time to find Argyll.

Carpark Ambush

That Albert failed to understand the simple dynamics of a contact group and how to use it came as no surprise to the four young people keeping his company.

"You have to select an individual contact from within the group," Donna pointed out, her voice an apology of sorts because she didn't want to make it sound like she thought Albert was stupid.

Albert frowned while Donna tried to explain something far too technical for his brain to comprehend.

"And that's not what I did?" he asked, already knowing the answer.

"That would be my guess," she shrugged.

Toby said, "You told us your granddaughter lumped all your new contacts from your travels into one group?"

He nodded, "Yes. I didn't know that would mean I sent the same message to everyone."

All four of his friends nodded their heads.

Asim said, "You have to pick one and open a message just to them, Bruv."

Albert heard his words but was too busy considering the ramifications of his message to respond. He'd sent it to everyone. Just how many people did that mean? How many would come? How many tried to contact his children?

With a mental shrug, he gave up trying to guess if there were a dozen more people heading his way and fished out his wallet.

Donna asked, "Aren't you going to check your phone to see who replied? What about your children? You wanted them to come here. Don't you need to see if they are on their way?"

Albert scratched his skull, thinking about whether it would be safe to put the chip back in his phone.

He shook his head. "I think it's probably safe to assume my kids are doing something. It would seem I orchestrated them getting the same message from about a dozen different sources. They will have a plan in action. I cannot guess what that is, but if I turn on my phone again and start making calls or responding to messages, the police in charge of the manhunt for me will come. They will come in numbers so whatever it is that my clever, brilliant kids are trying to do, I have to give them the space and freedom to do it."

"But what if ..." Donna persisted.

Albert cut her off, "But what if they are trying to get more information from me? But what if they need to ask me something important? You're right. By not speaking to them, I might be hampering their progress, but I know how bright they all are. They will find a way to succeed."

Asim held out his mobile. "Can't you just use my phone, Bruv?"

Albert placed a gentle hand on the young man's shoulder. "I'm afraid that would be just the same as using my own. They will be tracking their phones too. It's time to get moving," he announced, taking out some notes to tuck under his saucer. "I'll get breakfast," he looked around to see if anyone would argue.

Getting to her feet, Donna asked, "Where are you guys parked? We found a carpark around the back."

Asim pulled his coat on. It was a shiny silver thing that matched his ball cap with a motif that bragged 'Hood Style'. With his phone between his teeth to fight with his zip, he mumbled, "We're in the same place."

As it happened, Toby was parked right next to Asim, their cars two of only a dozen in a carpark that would fit more than a hundred.

"Where did you say we have to go?" Donna paused in front of Toby's car.

Albert looked from one car to the other. Toby drove a tiny Nissan Micra. It was rusty and had a fresh dent in the front left quarter panel, but the tyres were newish and it had five doors. That was a lot more than could be said for Asim's purple rocket which he drove like it was the space shuttle trying to reach escape velocity. It went airborne twice on the short drive from Glan-Y-Wern. All Asim needed was a small bump in the road to achieve some air time.

"I'll show you," he volunteered. "The boys can follow."

A voice from behind stopped his feet before they could move.

"Not so fast."

Everyone spun around to see who was there. The two men from the café were standing three yards away, handguns pointing at Albert and his group.

"You're Albert Smith, right?" said the one on the left. His name was Brad Richards. He wore his jacket with the sleeves pushed up to his elbows to show off his forearms. Brad liked his forearms. In the summer, he would wear a tight t-shirt to show off the rest of his torso, but that was impractical in the cold weather.

Albert took a second to debate his answer. The two men facing him were carbon copies of all the other Gastrothief agents he'd come across. He could lie to them; say he was

Reverend Roy Hope, but the likelihood they chose not to believe him and took them all for a little ride anyway was too great.

"I am," he replied. "There's no need to involve anyone else. These young people are just some folks I met this morning. They don't need to be a part of this."

"Yeah, right," spat Brad's companion, Garth. "That's why you had breakfast with them and were deep in conversation like you were old friends."

Albert cursed himself for being so unobservant. The men must have been in the café at the same time, yet he failed to notice them.

Brad motioned with his gun. "All of you. In the van."

A white transit van sat with its backdoors pointing their way.

Donna looked around for anyone who could help. She was not alone, but Garth cut her off before she could do anything that might draw attention.

"If I even think you are going to shout or scream, I will shoot the others, little girl."

"Not Albert though," Brad made sure his partner was on the same page. "We need to take him with us, right."

Albert narrowed his eyes and asked a question.

"You both work for the earl then, yes?"

"That's right," said Brad without thinking.

Garth tutted and slapped Brad's shoulder. "Nice one, dummy. That's operational security in practice right there."

While Brad's cheeks coloured for giving any sensitive information, Garth sneered and reiterated the need to get in the van.

Albert filed away the snippet of detail. It didn't mean much. Not at this stage. However, if he could get a message to someone, perhaps he could make sure the earl – whoever he was – met with justice after all.

At the back of the van Garth grabbed Donna roughly by the arm and poked his gun between her shoulder blades.

"Phones now, all of you. Or the girl gets it right here and now."

"Where are you taking us?" Afshin posed the question everyone wanted to ask. Like his cousin, he was looking for an opening. He knew, though, that ninja skills against guns has a low success rate. Bullets are just faster.

Brad collected the phones, trusting the threat against the girl would keep the men compliant. "To meet our employer." It was a cryptic reply that told them nothing.

Albert knew though. He was going to meet the Gastrothief and the only thought going through his head when they forced his friends into the van at gunpoint, was for his dog. Where was Rex and what was he doing?

On the other side of the carpark, hidden in a shadow and unseen by anyone, three pairs of eyes watched and calculated. No one spoke, but a tongue flicked out to taste the air.

Incandescent Rage

The earl was incandescent, his rage reaching levels even those closest to him had never seen before.

"A dog! A dog you say!"

"Yes, Sir," mumbled Chef Billy. His right leg hurt so much from where the dog hit him that he truly wondered if something might be broken. He didn't dare complain though. The earl's rage was legendary. So much so that Chef Billy's legs were shaking. It wasn't fear that caused the muscular tremors, but the certain knowledge that he needed to act if he was going to survive the next five minutes.

Earl Bacon's breath came in huffs, in and out through his nose as he fought to understand what he was being told. Years of planning to get the natural catacombs and caverns beneath his land converted into a biome where he could hide from the end of the world, the sale of his family's precious stately home to fund the project when his cashflow ran dry, months of operations to stock the larders, get the fields and farming projects running and to gather the people he needed to ensure his years below ground would be bountiful and blessed, and his own chef now claimed a dog had ruined one of his most irreplaceable supplies!

A chill stopped his heart and he clutched at his chest. Swivelling to face the sweating, shaking chef, his piggy eyes grew wide with horror.

"What sort of dog was it?"

No one spoke; all eyes on Chef Billy Gordon.

"Um, I'm not sure," he mumbled, his lips failing to operate as they should. "A big one for sure."

From just outside the doorway, drawn to see how the drama would pan out, and interested to witness Chef Billy's embarrassment since he'd refused her advances and was clearly either gay or blind, Sabrina said, "It was a German Shepherd."

Earl Bacon exploded. "What! A German Shepherd? A German Shepherd is inside my home?"

With everyone distracted, Chef Billy convinced himself this was his best chance. Ladd and Evan were in the kitchen but neither had their weapons drawn. Ladd was paying no attention and his gun was right there. Billy knew all he had to do was grab it and he could … what? Shoot Evan, shoot the earl, shoot anyone who got in his way and run hell for leather for the exit. He'd shoot the guards there too if he had to. He could make it.

Feeling his consciousness swim from the terror he felt, Chef Billy snatched at a large kitchen knife. The earl had his back exposed facing Sabrina in the hallway outside, but he could wait – the earl was the least important target.

With a scream of terrified rage meant to bolster his courage, Chef Billy swung the knife toward Ladd's neck. One strike was all it would take. The man would fall, and Billy knew the earl's bulbous body would protect him for the two seconds he needed to snatch the gun from Ladd's holster.

A shot rang out, deafening in the steel-walled room.

Billy slumped and fell, collapsing dead to the cold tile.

Tanya switched her chewing gum from one side of her mouth to the other, peered at Chef Billy to make sure her shot had been true, then placed her handgun away once more, enjoying the warmth under her left armpit as it radiated from the barrel.

"You're welcome," she winked at Ladd.

Everyone else was stunned, Earl Bacon most especially who was clutching his chest again. Sabrina's mouth hung open in a shocked but silent scream, her hands gripping either side of her face. She thought Billy would get a dressing down, not shot in the head.

"You shot him!" The earl pointed out what was thoroughly obvious.

Tanya's response was bored and dismissive. "He was about to stab Ladd in the neck."

The earl took a step back, getting his shoes away from the expanding pool of blood. "But ... but you shot him. He's *my* chef!"

"Was your chef," Tanya corrected. "Weren't you going to have me kill him anyway?"

"No!"

Tanya shrugged. "Oops. Like I said, he was going to stab Ladd. I didn't exactly have time to negotiate."

Earl Bacon squinted at Tanya. She was a good operative, but this was unacceptable. "So what if he was? I can replace Ladd tomorrow."

"Hey," Ladd frowned.

Paying his employee no mind, the earl continued. "One steroid abusing henchman is much the same as any other."

Ladd's frown deepened. "I'm standing right here, you know."

Wheeling around, though it took him a while and the effect of the motion was lost by the time he came to face Ladd, the earl snapped, "Are you going to cook my meals now? Are you? Do you know how to make roast asparagus au gratin, hmm? Do you know how to roast a guinea fowl to perfection? Chef Gordon was one in a million. Not least because he understood the impending cataclysm the world faces and wanted to be here. I didn't even have to pay him unlike you gun-toting yobs!"

The earl was upset and lashing out. He twisted around to aim an insult at Tanya only to find she had already wandered away.

Snarling through clenched teeth, he faced Ladd and Evan again.

"Get everyone. That dog must be found. I'll bet every penny I've got that it's the same damned dog that belongs to Albert Smith. If the dog is here, then so is that wretched old man. I want them both found. I want to know how they got in and I want to kill them myself. Do you hear? Find them and bring them to me!"

The Residents of Zion

R ex didn't need long to find people. He didn't even need his nose; he could see them. He bypassed the children who squealed with delight to see a dog. Knowing they would be no help, he kept going.

The fields of crops – vegetables, fruit trees, grape vines, corn, wheat, and many other foods surrounded what many might describe as a settlement. The residents called it Zion after the city in the film *The Matrix* simply because it was below ground. It had running water and due to the cave would never be cold, but there was no electricity and no modern devices. To wash their clothes, the captives, or 'saved', as the earl insisted they be called, would take their laundry to a drop off point. In labelled bags, their clothes, bedding, towels, or whatever, would vanish through a chute and be ready for collection two days later.

Shut off from the social network, television, and any form of news, the captives endured a basic life. It was uncomplicated, but there were medical facilities if needed. They couldn't get out though and other than new people arriving sporadically over the last six months or more – the earliest arrivals hadn't thought to keep track of days and below ground with no sun, it was nigh impossible anyway – they received no word of what might be happening in the world outside.

Shouts of a dog loose in the community spread fast, like the panicked word of a fire in a high-rise building.

Rex spotted an adult, a woman, and bounded to her, wagging his tail madly. She was just leaving her chicken coop and misinterpreted his excitement.

Squawking loudly, she yelled for help, her noise startling the chickens who in turn made a racket.

Confused at the female human's reaction, Rex altered course, this time heading for a man.

"Where's he come from?" bellowed a voice. It came from behind Rex, the humans reacting as one to catch the unexpected animal in their midst.

Another shouted, "Must be from the accommodation."

"It'll be the earl's dog," shouted another. "Must have gotten loose." Benny had no love of dogs and took a small knife from his belt. He saw a chance to strike back at his overlord and stuff the consequences.

Rex went from one person to the next finding they all shied away or tried to corral him. Two humans appeared with blankets in their hands, spread wide to form barriers. He had to dart away when one leapt, trying to ensnare him with the cloth.

Becoming frightened and most definitely annoyed, Rex barked a warning.

"How stupid are you lot? My human is here. He's come to deal with Tanya. I think" Rex added, still not one hundred percent on the mission objectives. It didn't matter. *He* could focus on Tanya, and it gave him an easy task to complete. She was dangerous and criminal. Rex could stop her. End of conversation. "I need to find a human called Argyll," he barked. "I can smell him. If you just get out of my way, I will find him for myself."

The humans were closing in though, more of them grabbing sheets or blankets. Rex barked his confusion and spun on the spot, ducking and weaving as he looked for a way to get through the circular barrier now closing in around him.

Benny wondered what his fellow captives might say when he stabbed the dog, but he didn't let it worry him much. If it belonged to the earl or anyone living in the 'accommodation' the term they gave to the palatial environment beyond the steel doors they could never open, then it deserved to die.

Poised to dive onto the struggling animal the moment the blankets covered it, he believed he could stab the dog multiple times without anyone even knowing it was him. So many limbs fumbling to hold the dog in place, who could ever know what had happened?

Rex's barks turned to threatening snarls – the humans were not listening. He was used to their species acting stupidly, but this was a new level.

Picking a target, Rex hunched his body, loading his legs ready to spring. One man didn't have a blanket. He was standing next to another who did, but this one held something in his hand. Rex recognised the danger. He would bite the arm that held whatever it was he sought to conceal.

Ready to launch his offensive, Rex watched everyone pause when a new voice boomed over all the others.

"Stop!"

A beat passed.

"Rex?" Argyll could scarcely believe his eyes.

The scent of the man he knew jerked Rex around, his snarl dropping when he finally met a friendly face.

Argyll rushed forward. "Oh, my God!"

Rex jumped up on his back legs, wiggling his butt with his front paws on Argyll's chest as he tried to get to the man's face with his tongue.

Twisting to meet the eyes of the people around him, Argyll blurted, "This is the dog I told you about." Meeting confused expressions, he said, "Don't you remember? The old man and the dog?"

Benny couldn't believe his ears. "What? You're starting all that nonsense again? I've had it up to here," he raised his hand above his head, "with your rubbish about some old man coming to save us all."

Argyll asked, "Is that a knife in your hand, Benny?"

Benny's guilty hand whipped behind his back whereupon he stuffed the knife back into his belt, cutting his skin and wincing in the process.

"No, what knife? No idea what you are talking about. Anyway, that dog must have come from the accommodation. I'll bet it belongs to the earl himself. We can use it to make demands."

"Yeah," echoed roughly half the crowd.

Argyll looked around until he found Sarah. They had formed a bond in the weeks since she was dragged here from Kent. It would have turned into something more had they not been captives and they both knew it. He befriended and comforted her the night she arrived.

"Sarah, do you remember the name of the dog?" Argyll prayed she could recall it now when he needed her to.

Sarah bit her bottom lip and strained to remember. She was about to shake her head and apologise when it popped into her brain.

"Rex Harrison!" she exclaimed excitedly. "I remember because he's an old film star."

Argyll gripped Rex's collar, placing his palm under the dangling pendant so all could see.

"Would anyone care to read what it says here?"

David Merchant, another of the wine growers from Kent was closer than Sarah and ready to hear some good news. He stepped forward to read the tag.

Nodding his head, he announced to the crowd. "It says 'Rex Harrison' just like Argyll said."

Benny didn't care. "Oh, so what? For all we know Argyll is a plant. He could be here just to spy on us and make sure we don't get any ideas in our heads about rising up."

A few folks made questioning faces, but it was Sarah who pointed out the incongruity first.

"But Argyll *is* the one inciting an uprising, Benny."

Heads turned to look Benny's way.

"Yeah, well maybe it's a clever double bluff," he offered. No one bought it.

Debbie, one of the older women in the community and one who had children trapped with her, had gravitated naturally toward the position of matriarch. In her early fifties, children had come late and after much struggling. She wanted them to see the sun again.

Stepping forward, she asked, "What does this mean, Argyll? Is there really someone on the outside trying to help us?"

"Yeah?" Karl Fielding, the most recent arrival, raised his voice. "No one out there knows anything about us. It's not in the papers or anything." He'd been taken just less than a week ago, ripped from his bakery in Lyme Regis mere days before the Gastrothief story broke.

Argyll nodded his head, acknowledging an inescapable point, but argued, "One man knows, and he's travelling with this dog. If Rex is here, then Albert cannot be far away."

Questions abounded but they were all cut off by the sound of the public address system echoing through the settlement.

"ALBERT SMITH, IF YOU ARE LISTENING, IF YOU MANAGED TO GAIN ENTRY TO THE BIOME, WE ARE COMING FOR YOU. SURRENDER AND NO ONE WILL BE HURT."

"Except him," sniggered a voice in the background.

"SHUTTUP!" hissed the original voice. "ALBERT SMITH WE ARE COMING FOR YOU."

"What if he's not there?" asked the second voice.

The first said, "Oh, cripes, I hadn't thought of that."

Bemused, Argyll and the residents of the settlement waited for the announcement to end.

"RIGHT, ALBERT SMITH IF YOU ARE NOT THERE TO HEAR THIS ... Oh, dang it, that doesn't work, does it." Beginning to sound flustered, the booming voice gave it one last go. "RESIDENTS OF ZION, GATHER IN THE CENTRE OF THE SETTLEMENT. BE READY TO HAND OVER THE DOG." There was a pause before the voice added, "AND ALBERT SMITH IF HE IS THERE."

The Penny Drops

A little more than a mile away in the village of Glan-Y-Wern, Curtis Jones was on his way to the post office and general store. The presence of unexpected visitors had not gone unnoticed though no one knew who they were or what might have brought them to such a quiet corner of Wales, and though several people had approached the newcomers, no answers had been given.

Shelley claimed she approached a group of people who arrived in Range Rovers and a van. She said they were all pleasant enough but wouldn't tell her why they were there. In fact, according to Shelley, they were all rather tight lipped.

Curtis thought he knew though. A sneaky peek around the corner was all he needed – they were a film crew. They'd come early and there was an attractive young woman wearing smart clothes. Curtis was willing to bet money she was Marissa Cardheart, the PR woman from head office in London.

They'd dropped everything to be here this morning.

She wasn't answering her phone today. Not that she was answering it yesterday either - she was the one who made the calls, not the one who received them. Her cryptic manner yesterday had to be all to do with the winner in the village. They wanted a big public announcement and were going to make a huge song and dance about tracking down the winner.

Why the secrecy?

Because they didn't want a dozy Welshman with his Welsh accent messing things up. That's why. Curtis was hopping mad about it. It wasn't so much the underhandedness of it; cutting him out when he was the one holding the ticket, the one who met the winner. It was the subterfuge with which they deployed their tactics.

If Marissa told him she needed to do things this way, he would have played along.

Curtis took a mental pause to admit that, actually, he wouldn't have done any such thing. He would have found a way to be part of the proceedings because he got paid on commission and had stayed awake last night mentally spending the uplift in wages.

Puffing out his cheeks to let a breath of exasperation flap his lips on the way out, Curtis pushed his way through the post office door.

He was buying cigarettes, something Mrs Jones didn't know about. He always paid cash, always bought a ten pack and smoked two a day, both before lunchtime so his breath would be clear of the stink by the time he got home.

It had been that way since before they got married four years ago.

What Curtis did not know was that his wife knew precisely what he did every day and had been holding the information in reserve like any clever wife until the day she needed it most.

Tearing the cellophane cover from the box, and the gold foil piece folded over the cigarettes inside, Curtis proceeded to extract his early morning smoke from the packet on his way from the shop. Preoccupied with thought of Marissa 'ruddy' Cardheart, he fumbled the white cylinder of death.

Attempts to catch it almost snapped the delicate tube in half, so Curtis let it fall. Coming down to one knee to collect it, his eyes alighted upon the cover of a national magazine. He recognised the name – everyone knew it from a big political scandal they exposed a few years ago. He'd never read a copy, nor even held one, but these were not the thoughts going through his head.

Staring out from the cover was a slightly younger version of the old vicar who came into his shop yesterday. The old vicar with the winning ticket.

Ripping the post office's remaining copy of The Independent Enquirer from the shelf, Curtis confirmed there was nothing wrong with his eyes. The man's name really was Albert Smith, the name of the person who bought the ticket in Melton Mowbray. He might have given a false name when he came into the shop, but there was no crime in that. Curtis had been worried the winner was a crook who stole or otherwise came by the betting slip Albert Smith placed. That wasn't the case, but the truth was no better.

If anything it was worse.

"Here, this isn't a library," complained Gareth from behind the post office counter. "Are you going to pay for that?"

Curtis didn't even hear him speak. The report said Albert Smith was a wanted man. That was as far as he read. Had his eyes tracked a few lines further he would have discovered the debate suggesting the opposite ought to be true, but he didn't. He didn't need to. The moment he started reading, his brain connected the dots in his head – he knew the name and the story. The man was a wanted terrorist!

Curtis Jones, manager of the Glan-Y-Wern branch of Grand's Turf Accountants unthinkingly committed the crime of shoplifting when he ran from the premises.

At the payphone on the corner – he didn't dare use his own, Curtis pressed the nine button three times. When the call ended, he was surprised at how spent he felt – utterly drained. Knowing what he now did, Curtis was certain Albert Smith wasn't coming forward to collect his money. He was going to get caught and go to jail – the cops were already on their way courtesy of his anonymous call.

All he had to do now was get to work and make the stub from Albert Smith's bet disappear. They could yell at him, they could go nuts, but they couldn't prove he still had it. A few months from now, many, many miles from Glan-Y-Wern, a man was going to quietly cash in the winning bet.

Scotland, perhaps, Curtis thought to himself. He'd never been. He would book a big room somewhere posh and take his wife. His eyes flared with a new idea: maybe with all the money he could afford a new wife.

Buoyed by the ideas now crowding his head, Curtis scurried off to his place of work.

Roadside Recovery

Albert was getting jaw ache from gritting his teeth. It was one thing to run out of luck and find himself in a terrible predicament – it wasn't his first time – another entirely to drag other people down with him.

They were all so young. Heck Donna and Toby were still school age though he knew both had left at the earliest opportunity to work in their family businesses.

On the plus side they were being taken to the Gastrothief's lair and he was going to get to meet the shadowy character he'd been tailing for the last few months. On the downside, he knew the Gastrothief employed killers like Tanya and Baldwin. It would take mere moments to realise the kids in Albert's company served no purpose.

As for him, Albert didn't fancy his chances one bit. Without Rex to help, what could he do to prevent the inevitable?

With Brad driving, Garth was twisted around in the front passenger seat to aim his gun loosely at the five people stuffed into the back of the van. They had no seats, not so much as a blanket or a toolbox. Forced to sit uncomfortably on the hard floor, it further tipped the advantage in their captor's favour.

Asim and Afshin were exchanging glances, attempting to wordlessly formulate some kind of plan to escape. Albert watched them knowing to try anything would be foolhardy.

They could not hope to get to Garth and disarm him before he started shooting and they were all like fish in a barrel in the back of the van.

Toby and Donna were holding hands, the teenage couple keeping close for the comfort it gave.

"Are you seeing this?" Brad asked, distracting Garth momentarily.

Garth checked his passengers, narrowing his eyes at each of them in warning before risking a quick glance through the windshield.

Albert looked too. There was a motorcycle and side car blocking the road. It looked to be broken down. Or crashed perhaps. He'd seen it a few minutes ago, just as they were leaving the main road from Abergowd-Coed to Glan-Y-Wern. Confirming he'd been searching in the right place when he lost Rex, the van took the narrow track that skirted the coast and it was then that the motorcycle had roared past them.

Albert assumed it was going to the same place, the passenger undoubtedly one of the Gastrothief's employees. Yet half a mile later it was broken down in the middle of the road and the person riding it was waving an arm to flag down the next vehicle to come along.

Squinting through the windscreen, Albert stared at the person. It was a woman. Not a young woman and there was something disturbingly familiar about her. The helmet obscured her face almost completely even though the visor was flipped up.

Brad slowed.

"Looks like an old lady," he muttered. "I'm just going to move her and the bike out of the way."

Garth turned back to watch Albert and the kids again, his gun never wavering or wobbling.

"Don't be too long. I'll miss you," Garth quipped, sharing a joke with his colleague. Otherwise neither man said a word.

Albert kept watching.

With the door closed it wasn't possible to hear what Brad said to the person in motorcycle leathers, nor hear what might have been said in return. However, he saw the stun gun abruptly appear from behind her back and the shocked faces of his friends when they saw her jam it under Brad's chin.

The Gastrothief's henchman collapsed like a sack of bricks, hitting the tarmac like someone had cut the power to all the muscles keeping him upright. Essentially, that was precisely what had just happened.

Garth didn't see it and wasn't going to be fooled by the 'eyes agog' expressions he was getting from his captives. So far as he was concerned, they were trying to pull the old 'look behind you' trick. What amateurs. Who did they think they were messing with?

His head twitched sharply left when the old lady rapped her knuckles on his window.

"What the?"

Raising her voice to be heard, she shouted, "Your friend collapsed. I think he might be having a heart attack. Can you help?"

Growling at the people tucked out of sight in the back of the van, Garth said, "Don't anybody move a muscle. Do and I'll shoot you."

Presented with a problem – a glance showed Brad flat out on his back in the road – Garth wasn't sure what to do. He couldn't get out of the van because he had prisoners who would attempt to flee the moment he did. Obviously, he couldn't stay in the van either because the road was blocked. If he tried to drive, the prisoners would once again attempt to escape, this time by overpowering him while his attention was on the road.

He was going to have to call for help. Annoying because he had been looking forward to presenting the earl with the man he'd been after for weeks. Taking out his phone, a smile crossed his face. He was going to call Tanya. She was the one tasked with capturing Albert Smith. Maybe she would be amenable to a date in exchange for the old man. Goodness knows she refused everyone else's advances. Scoring a date with Tanya, who was one hot piece of fluff in Garth's books, would give him hero status among the lads.

Flicking his eyes between the phone and the people in the back of the van, he was about to select her contact when the old lady thumped on the window again, this time using her fist.

"Hey! Can you hear me? Your friend needs help."

With an annoyed grimace, he reached across to power down the window. He was going to shoot the old lady; no one would hear it way out here.

However, as the window came down, the woman dropped her hand, fumbling with something she was holding out of sight in the other. When the gap got big enough for Garth to shoot through without risking blasting out the window, he lifted his gun hand to switch targets. It would only take but a second, but in the heartbeat between looking away from her to check his captives, and looking back, she had lifted her arms and was throwing something in through his window.

The something turned out to be a cat.

An angry cat.

It landed on Garth's face like one of those things from the *Alien* movies, spitting and hissing and clawing like mad to get away. Right before the shocked eyes of Albert's companions, it ran up Garth's face, eighteen tiny claws gouging furrows in his skin.

Garth squealed, the noise a mixture of terror and pain. He hadn't seen what the old lady threw. But he did know there was something on his face. It was cutting out the light and it was trying to kill him.

His gun went off, a hole appearing in the roof of the van right above his head.

A second had passed, no more, but that was enough time for Albert to react. Convinced he knew who the old lady driving the motorcycle and sidecar was before she spoke, any doubt got swept away when she did.

He met Gloria in Dundee when the former police undercover operative carefully and cleverly manipulated him into helping her solve a crime. She was in her eighties and just as dangerous, if a little slower, than she had been fifty years ago.

Albert dived to get to Garth's gun hand. The cat to the face might have shocked the man, but it wouldn't take him long to recover. When he did, he would be hopping mad and looking for blood.

With a banshee cry of, "Get him!", Albert gripped Garth's meaty forearm. He wasn't strong enough to disarm the Gastrothief's agent, but that was okay because help arrived an instant later.

Asim, Afshin, and not to be outdone, both Toby and Donna dived onto one of the flailing henchman.

Watching through the open window, Gloria chuckled at Albert's antics before asking, "Have you lot got his weapon yet?"

Asim ripped the handgun from Garth's grip. "Got it!"

Garth was screaming obscenities and promising horrendous violence the moment he was able to get up.

The cat was on the dashboard, preening itself with a disinterested paw.

Gloria raised the stun gun again. "Ready?"

Albert let go of Garth, easing slowly into the back of the van again. One by one the others let go too until it was just Asim and Afshin holding him down.

With a nod, they jumped back in unison. With a roar, Garth sat up and Gloria said, "Goodnight," as she jammed the stun gun through the window and into his rising forehead.

There was a spark and a 'zzzzzt' sound. Garth crumpled just like Brad.

Talking in a tone that suggested events were nothing more than business as usual, Gloria said, "Well, don't just sit there you lot. Get out. We need to tidy these two away. I can't do it myself. Not at my age." Looking directly at Asim she pointed a bony finger. "You and you," she included Afshin, "strip them both. Everything I mean."

Asim swung his head around to stare at Albert, his eyes twice the size they ought to be.

"Bruv, is that your wife or something?"

Albert chuckled and began to clamber over the front seat to get out.

"Not my wife, no, Asim." Outside on the road he pulled Gloria into a hug.

"You're going to tell me I sent you a message last night, right?"

Gloria's eyebrows waggled in question. "That's right. The one about getting a message to your children and then coming here? Was I not supposed to get it?"

Albert released her from his embrace. "Not exactly, no. I'm very glad to see you though. How did you know we were in the back or were you just randomly hijacking transit vans today?"

Gloria reached up to accept her cat, Tabatha, when Asim climbed out of the van holding it. With a quick thank you to Asim, she said, "I saw them take you in the carpark."

Asim had been about to turn around to help his cousin and Toby drag Garth's unconscious body from the passenger's seat when he heard what Gloria said.

"And you didn't think to interrupt them then?" he said aghast.

Gloria shot him a look that questioned his intelligence. "How would that help you find the hidden lair of the Gastrothief?" Turning to Albert she said, "I assume that's where they were taking you."

Albert could only agree. "That would be my guess too."

"Do you really want us to strip these two naked?" asked Donna, clearly not excited at the prospect of undressing either man.

Gloria nudged her out of the way. "I'll do it if the rest are you are too squeamish. Blokes will happily run around in just their underpants. I speak from experience though when I say they are most reluctant to do the same with their tackle on display."

"Experience?" Donna questioned.

Asim, kneeling in the front of the van still, stopped manhandling Garth's head to ask, "How much experience are we talking about?"

Cackling, Gloria was speaking to Albert when she said, "The young always act as if they invented sex. You," she pointed at Asim, "give his legs a yank. "And you," she aimed the finger at Afshin. "Stop trying to cradle his head." Grabbing hold of Garth's jeans, Gloria leant her muscle to the task, the henchman's body zipping out into free space for the briefest of moments before gravity claimed it.

He hit the ground with a crunch, a soft moan escaping his lips before he farted loudly.

Gloria, all business, laughed despite herself and asked, "Did someone step on a duck?"

Albert meanwhile crossed to Brad taking Toby and Donna with him.

"Shouldn't we ... I dunno, like check he's ok or something first?" asked Toby. "Is he even alive?"

Albert stuck two fingers on Brad's neck.

"He's alive." Tugging the man's belt off, he added, "The thing to remember ... two things actually." Albert held up his right hand and used the left to fold in his index finger. "One: Henchmen are by definition subhuman. Whatever you do to them, there's never a reason to feel bad about it. Two: If he wakes up, he'll likely kill us all."

Startled into motion by Albert's revelation, Toby ripped Brad's coat open. Donna was pulling off his shoes.

"Here, use these," Gloria tossed Albert some sturdy zip ties. "And this." She threw him a length of cord.

Donna screwed her face up in horror. "What do we use the cord for?"

Gloria looked like it pained her to have to explain everything. "You use the zip ties to bind their ankles and wrists, then pull both back and link them together with the cord. Haven't you ever hogtied a person before?"

Seeing Donna's expression, Albert took the implements from her. "Don't worry, I've got it."

Two minutes later, Brad and Garth were off the road and out of sight in a shallow depression. Gloria assured everyone they would work themselves free in a few hours. It would take them that long to accept they could do so by dislocating a shoulder or stripping all the skin from their ankles as they fought themselves free from the plastic ties.

"Right?" Gloria clapped her hands together to get everyone's attention. "Shall we find the entrance to this secret lair then?"

The Gathering

In the Glan-Y-Wern harbour, the woman Curtis took to be Marissa Cardheart found herself being approached by a young man. Her name wasn't Marissa though it was Jessica. Jessica Fletcher. Like so many others, she received an unexpected message from Albert late the previous evening. Reading it with her eyes flitting rapidly across the screen and her heart beating double time, she knew precisely what it meant: Opportunity.

Returning from dropping Albert in Cornwall almost a week earlier, she'd spent the entire return trip going over the incredible story Albert insisted was true. Her quest to prove it all began the moment she got home, and she had a small team working on it within the hour.

Convincing her editor to give her the resources she needed proved tougher than she expected. A former senior police detective forced to operate on his own because the police wouldn't listen? A master criminal operating a small army of agents charged with kidnapping and stealing? Bombs, murders, two old men flying a fighter plane from the Second World War to prevent a crime from happening while all the time the man at the centre of it was being pursued by the police?

It was sensational. It was explosive. It would sell a bucketload of copies whether there was a true word in it or not. The Independent Enquirer was all about its reputation though. A bad story might cripple its viability to continue selling and she had to convince her editor every word was indeed accurate.

Albert Smith, at that point the most wanted man in Britain, was innocent of all charges. Not only that, the former senior police detective was closing in on the biggest secret for decades: a hidden network of agents working to kidnap people from the food industry. No one knew about them, just a widowed old man touring the country with his dog.

Brow-beaten into listening when Jessica called in some of her colleagues who had already researched small elements of the story and had what amounted to evidence of sorts, the editor contacted a source high up in the Metropolitan Police who immediately scoffed at the idea.

However, when Jessica's editor carefully slipped in the word 'Gastrothief' his contact didn't question it. Instead, he said it was the daft ramblings of an old and soon to be disgraced police officer. In so doing he proved one thing unequivocally: there was a story.

Staking his future on the story, he gave Jessica the go ahead to write it, but it needed to be done fast. Three days later, they published. He'd known her a while and she was the kind of reporter that only came along once in a generation. The kind of journalist who possessed an uncanny ability to find the truth and combined it with a sense of reckless risk one might otherwise find only in pirates and special forces soldiers.

For her part, Jessica Fletcher felt like she'd been holding her breath for a week when the message from Albert flashed into her phone. Two minutes later she was talking to her editor again. None of them had predicted the upwelling of public support that followed their story. Now Jessica had a once in a lifetime opportunity to see the tale through to its conclusion. It would be the biggest news story in years. It would be global, and they were going to be the only reporters at the scene.

They chose to set up in the carpark next to the harbour using the old trick of 'right of press' when a woman with windswept ruddy cheeks approached to ask what they were doing. That was when Jessica first spotted the young black man.

He was watching her group with a curious look. Jessica guessed he was a local and thought nothing further until she found he was coming her way. He'd been talking with the harbour master, Shelley Rankin – Jessica recorded her name as any reporter would.

"Hello," Oxford Shaw extended his hand as he came toward the woman who appeared to be in charge. Several of her colleagues looked up to see who had spoken before returning to their tasks. "I'm Oxford. Are you here to cover a story?"

Jessica tucked a stray piece of hair behind her ear, cursing herself for not bringing a hat or a scarf. How to answer? She could deflect by saying she wasn't at liberty to reveal any details at this time, but there was something about the man. It took her a second, but the spark of realisation almost made her jump.

"Oxford Shaw?" she asked, catching the young man completely off guard. "Constable Oxford Shaw from Stilton?" She had hold of his hand and hadn't let go. Doing so now that his grip had gone slack from being thrown off balance, she plucked her phone from a trouser pocket.

Oxford mumbled, "Um, yes?"

It was clear he was about to ask how she knew him, so Jessica filled in the blanks.

"I'm Jessica. I met Albert in Eton. We spoke on the phone." When she started researching Albert's story, it had taken her all of five minutes to track down a number for the police station in Stilton.

Shaking his head at the unlikely coincidence, Oxford said, "Goodness. Well it's good to meet you."

"I'm the reporter who broke the story. He messaged me last night begging that I send a message to his children in Kent, and he told me ..."

"That he's here in Glan-Y-Wern and believes the Gastrothief is too," Oxford finished her sentence.

They both stopped talking, their foreheads knitted in confusion.

"You got the same message," Jessica concluded. When Oxford nodded, she queried, "Why would Albert do that?"

All Oxford could do was shrug. Nodding his head toward the guys setting up cameras and the van with the satellite dish on its roof, he said, "I take it you're here in the hope he really has found the Gastrothief." He wanted to comment about how his part in the events in Stilton were very much downplayed in her article. Recognising it would be immature and pointless to do so, he let it go.

Thrusting her hands back into her pockets to keep them warm, Jessica said, "That's the plan. Also, though, to give Albert any help we can. When I met him, he was on the run; that's hardly something a man his age should have to endure. Especially when he's innocent." A new thought barged its way to the front of the queue. "You do believe that, don't you? You're not here to arrest him?"

Oxford snorted a breath at the suggestion. "Perish the thought. I would be dead if it were not for that man. And his dog. That reminds me. In his message, Albert said he'd lost Rex. Have you had an update from him at all?"

"No. Nothing," Jessica was sad about it. "He's not answering his phone. We're um ... we're about to start grilling the locals about him. He said he was here so someone must know where he is. It's not a big place, perhaps you would like to help."

"Here, is this about that Albert Smith character?" asked Shelley.

Neither Oxford nor Jessica had heard her approach, but she was standing just a few feet away.

Shelley nodded her head at Oxford. "That fella asked me about him. Old man pretending to be a vicar. Who is he really?"

"Pretending to be a vicar?" Jessica repeated.

"That's right. Had a dog collar and was asking about a local stately home and the bloke that owns it."

Jessica and Oxford turned toward each other, their eyes locking in the certain knowledge they were both thinking the same thing.

"The Gastrothief!"

Lost, Shelley said, "The gastro what?"

"The Gastrothief," said a new voice, the words followed a moment later by a man as he rounded the back of Jessica's car. "The slightly awkward yet fitting name Albert Smith gave to the person he is pursuing."

Shelley, Oxford and Jessica gawped at the newcomer. Who was he that he was so well informed? His accent was anything but local. English, but from one of the home counties. Most likely Kent, Jessica judged.

Dressed in a suit and tie, he wore a scruffy coat over the top that wasn't done up. In his mid-fifties, but looking a little older, his eyes bored into each of the three people to his front before he extended his hand to the youngest of them.

"Detective or uniform?" he asked. When Oxford allowed his arm to be pumped but gave no response because he was still trying to figure out what was going on, the man apologised. "Sorry, I can spot a fellow copper from a mile away. I'm Detective Sergeant Mike Atwell from Kent. I met Albert at a wedding of all places just after the debacle in Whitstable. I probably should have arrested him on the spot, but ... well, you gain a nose for these things over the years. Seems I was right to let him go."

Mike released Oxford's hand and offered it to Jessica. With introductions done, he said, "I believe I overheard you planning to scour the village looking for him?"

"Oh there's no need to do that," Shelley threw in her opinion. "He's staying at This-tle-Do-Me at the top of the hill. I can take you there if you like."

What the people in the harbour did not notice just before they turned to set off was the man watching them from his car. Chief Inspector Quinn had been about to exit his car when he saw DS Mike Atwell strolling across the carpark.

He'd been convinced his former sergeant had let Albert Smith go and though this didn't constitute proof, if he caught Atwell helping the fugitive now, he could have him charged and most likely sentenced. It wouldn't even matter if Albert Smith turned out to be innocent – a fugitive is a fugitive. DS Atwell's job was to arrest him on sight and though the man had quit and handed in his warrant card, he was technically still on the police payroll and therefore still technically a police officer. There was not one jot of grey area.

At the very least it would cost Atwell his pension.

Quinn knew his motivation was mostly revenge - Atwell stood up to him and made him look bad in front of his subordinates. Well, total career destruction plus criminal charges ought to remind everyone who the boss is.

He waited until DS Atwell and the people he was with left. They looked like reporters which made Quinn both wary and happy at the same time. If he could arrest Albert Smith or if Albert Smith was right about the whole thing and there was an even bigger fish to arrest, Quinn could get to the reporters first and be the face of the breaking story.

He needed to stay out of sight though. If Atwell saw him, it would change his behaviour and Quinn wanted to catch him aiding Albert Smith. When they were out of sight, he eased his car back out on the main road and drove up the hill. There would be somewhere to lie low for a while. A rarely travelled coastal road would do nicely.

At Gun Point

The residents of Zion were used to sporadic and unannounced visits from their guards or, at least, as used to something like that as a person could get. Only a very few of them had ever met the earl in person, but they all knew who was behind their captivity.

Not that he ever came down to the settlement or spoke to them over the address system. Those who met him did so in his palatial quarters, a sumptuous area of accommodation with every luxury a person could dream of. To get there, they were taken blindfolded so none could learn the layout of the accommodation. They knew that was the way to freedom, but even from the outside they could tell it was a labyrinth inside. Set over multiple levels, if ever they went close enough, clambering up the sloping cave wall to get to the accommodation, they could see their overlords passing by the small round windows that looked down upon the central cavern.

When they did get visitors, it was always the armed ones and they came because they needed something, never for anything good. There were scientific types working for the earl, men and women employed to monitor the environment inside the biome – it had to be right for growing crops and supporting livestock. How else was the earl going to stay well fed?

The scientists would come to take readings, check the growth of food crops against clever little charts which had no bearing on the reality of farming underground with artificial light. The armed guards kept watch and rarely was it that anyone spoke to the residents unless one of the scientists had a specific question.

Today there were no scientists and the armed guards, both men and women, were moving faster than normal. Not that there was any confusion as to why. Rex had arrived and the only way he could have entered the cavern was from the accommodation. They knew that for certain. Zion's residents had been all over every inch of the cavern: if there was a way out, they would have found it.

Of course, there actually was a way out but that meant going through the seawater pool which they were assured was blocked off with steel mesh. In theory, if they could hold their breath for long enough, they might be able to use their tools to cut a hole in it. However, more than one had tried, and all but one had died. The survivor, Argyll, only just made it back to the surface before his air ran out, and even then lost consciousness and had to be towed to shore.

The earl's armed thugs along with his less prone-to-violence security team who monitored and managed the installation's double width, double height, two-inch thick steel gate, had already torn through the accommodation to prove the dog wasn't there.

They couldn't figure out how he got in, but finding one of the doors leading to the captives and their settlement put the argument and accusations on hold for a while. If there was a door open, however unlikely it seemed that the dog could have operated the mechanism himself, then down with the captives was where he had to be.

Argyll, Sarah, and everyone else in Zion saw the armed guards coming almost from the moment they left the accommodation. With moments to spare and battling a difference of opinion that threatened to split the group, Argyll convinced the other residents of the need to hide Rex. Albert Smith was coming. He had to be. That meant they were going to be rescued. All they had to do was hang on and be ready. Above all, they had to protect Albert's dog.

With the guards jogging to get there quickly, Argyll led Rex around the back of their houses and across to the seawater pool. There, just a couple of yards above the high tide line, sat his smoke house. It had been built in anticipation of his arrival and completely stripped and rebuilt to meet Argyll's specification upon his arrival.

He made a lot of noise about how none of it was right: the equipment was wrong and needed to be replaced or re-engineered, the tables had to be moved from one side to the other because they were too close to the smoker itself ... the list went on. In truth, most of it was fine, but even before Argyll arrived in the underground cavern he knew he was going to try to escape. To achieve that was going to take planning and time.

He didn't know how much time, but guessing that he would need 'things' to aid his escape; contraband items such as rope or weapons, chemicals with which he might figure out how to make explosives, he envisaged also needing a place to keep them hidden. It was to that end he created the cubby hole behind the tables. No one knew it was there other than the two men who helped him create it.

It held a few things he believed might come in useful, but now it was to house something far more precious.

"You want me to go in there?" Rex asked, peering into the dark hole. "I'm not entirely convinced by this plan. How about we go with my plan and find a way out? The subpart of that plan is to bite anyone who gets in our way. See? Vastly superior to your plan." He lowered his backend to sit looking up at Argyll.

"I need to hide you," Argyll tried to explain. Using babyish language he said, "Bad men are coming."

Rex wagged his tail. "Yes, bad men. We should bite them. Well, I guess I should bite them. Humans are rubbish at biting. Maybe just hit them with something. Do you have any guns?"

Not even recognising that Rex was attempting to communicate, Argyll had carried on talking. "The bad men are looking for you. They might want to hurt you. I know you don't understand me ..."

"I do, actually."

"But it's important that you stay in here until I come for you. And you have to keep quiet. Can you do that?"

Rex peered into the hole again. With a huff of defeat, he conceded to Argyll's urgent motions and desperate tone. He didn't like the hole, but he couldn't get his point across, so for now at least, he accepted that he might as well do what Argyll asked.

Relieved to put the table back in place, effectively trapping Rex inside, Argyll repeated a promise to not be too long – a sentence that meant nothing to a dog – begged Rex to stay quiet and ran back to the centre hub of the settlement to join the others just as the earl's thugs were arriving.

Tanya was leading them. Argyll knew her from Arbroath and his ride from there to here. She'd been part of a two-person team who kidnapped him in broad daylight. Oddly, he hadn't seen the man she'd been with since.

Guns drawn – some of them were carrying snub nosed machine guns on shoulder straps – the thugs came into what might elsewhere pass for a village square. They did so from multiple angles to keep the residents off guard and force them to look in all directions. Their usual demeanour, while not friendly, was never aggressive. Today was different and everyone could feel it.

There were seven thugs; five men and two women, Kelly and Tanya. They were all lean, fit individuals with strong muscles and fast reflexes. The residents outnumbered them by more than ten to one just counting the adults, but armed with garden tools and a few small knives, any time the subject of rising up arose, it was quickly dismissed. Even if they succeeded, many would die and then what? The cavern was completely sealed. The only way out was through one of the doors into the accommodation and they were always locked from the inside.

No one spoke as the guards fanned out on one side of the captives. Tanya stopped short, nodding to a much larger man that he should proceed.

The man's name was Ryan. Among all the earl's agents, he stood out for having almost no ego. He cared not one bit that the person directing his actions was a petite woman who weighed less than he could bicep curl.

It made Tanya like him which, surprisingly, was not a deliberate tactic on his part.

Stepping forward, he cast his eyes down for a moment and pushed a hand clad in a fingerless tactical glove through the stubble he called a hairstyle. Looking back up, his piercing blue eyes swept from left to right across the villagers.

Forcing everyone to wait when they expected him to talk cranked the tension higher and made the captives even more nervous. Pausing here and there to linger with his intense gaze boring into those who looked most scared did the majority of his work, so when he cocked his Sig Sauer machine pistol a few whimpers escaped the assembly.

It made Tanya smile.

Finally Ryan spoke. "Who will I have to kill?"

No one spoke, but there were more fear-filled whimpers.

Ryan waited ten seconds before continuing. "As I am sure you already know, we are looking for a dog. He is here in the cavern and since I cannot see him, the only conclusion I can draw is that you have chosen to hide him. So I ask again, who will I have to kill?"

Argyll called out, "We all have vital roles. Which of us is expendable in the earl's eyes?"

Ryan chose not to answer, opting instead to watch. He wanted to see who was looking where: they would give themselves away without speaking.

"We haven't seen a dog," wailed Sarah, wishing her voice had come out stronger.

Tanya shot her a glare and smiled when she said, "We'll remember you said that."

No one else said anything, but they couldn't help glancing at certain members of their small community.

Though it wasn't exactly a blind threat, Ryan never intended to kill one of them. He doubted it would be necessary; the threat was enough. However, he would identify the guilty persons and make sure someone took a beating they would all remember. The Scotsman perhaps. Among all the villagers, he was the one man with a little backbone. Seeing him be taken down several pegs would serve as a timely lesson and keep the rest in place.

Turning his eyes away from the crowd for the first time, Ryan used his left hand to point at two of his colleagues.

"Her. The one who wants us to believe there is no dog. Bring her out. She will do." He'd seen Argyll look her way when she spoke, saw the expression in his eyes.

The crowd parted around Sarah when the two armed men came forward. Cleary petrified, she didn't move until they grabbed her arms and started to drag her forward.

Argyll's teeth ground against each other and his feet twitched but he didn't move. What was better? Life as a captive living below ground to do someone else's bidding or a quick death? Albert Smith was here, of that he remained certain. They just needed more time. If he gave up Rex, they would surely kill the dog, but what choice was he being given?

Benny yelled, "Argyll! Tell them where you hid it!"

There were a few gasps. Most from people who were relieved it wasn't them being threatened with on-the-spot execution. They didn't want to see Sarah die, but Argyll clearly knew something, so if this was their chance to escape and it cost Sarah's life, well it was a price they were willing to pay.

The armed men with Sarah were in front of the press of captives where she was on her knees. Now they were looking for further instruction, but Ryan wasn't meeting their eyes. He was looking at Argyll.

He waited.

He waited some more, Argyll returning Ryan's passive gaze with hate-filled eyes that might produce laser beams if he tried any harder.

STEVE HIGGS

With a small shrug that said, 'The ball is in your court', Ryan asked, "Are you going to wait until after I grow bored and have her shot before you tell me where the dog is?"

Argyll refused to look at Sarah; he knew he would cave if he saw her face. However, when one of the men holding her cocked his weapon, his resolve failed.

Ryan watched the change in the broad Scotsman's hard exterior and nodded to himself.

Addressing his colleagues, he said, "Stay here. Keep the rest of them in check. I will deal with the dog."

Tanya started walking toward Argyll. "I'll deal with the dog. I have a score to settle."

Ryan frowned for the first time since arriving at the settlement.

"The earl wants it alive."

Tanya kept walking, but turned around so she was going backward. Lifting her arms to either side in an expression of innocence, she shot him a wicked grin.

"He'll be alive. I'm just going to put a few holes in him." Spinning around just before she reached Argyll, she jabbed her gun into his ribs hard enough to draw a grunt of pain and with a growl demanded, "Show me."

Ryan followed her, mildly concerned for what she might do.

Argyll's brain worked at maximum speed, running through the inventory of items in his smokehouse. Was this the opportunity he'd been hoping for? It was one against two, but they were so supremely confident they would not be expecting him to attack. There were tools and things in the smokehouse, implements he could use to launch an offensive.

Away from the rest of the guards, whatever happened would not be seen. Sure, they would react when Tanya or Ryan got a shot off, but if he got it right, he would take out one of them before the other knew what was happening.

Then there was Rex.

He knew from Albert that his pet was a former police dog. He would know to attack, wouldn't he? Argyll wasn't certain and though he thought it likely, it wasn't a tactic he could rely upon.

No, he would have to do this himself. Picturing it in his head, he could pull the table away to reveal the hidden space behind it. At that moment when Tanya and Ryan were looking that way and not at him, he would strike.

All he had to do was act beaten and wait for his chance.

Revelations

Malory and Joshua gaped at the people on their driveway. Mouths open, they had no words with which to respond to the news.

Jessica begged, "How long ago did he leave?" Adding, "It's really important we find him," to prompt the couple into revealing everything they knew.

Malory looked over Jessica's head to the gathering behind her. There were close to twenty; she tried to do a count, but they kept moving around. She recognised more than half as villagers, some of which she knew by name, and some she did not.

The gaggle of people that left the harbour gained two more when Jason and Lilly Biggs spotted Shelley heading up the hill. They were just coming out of their front door and off to do their weekly shop at the big supermarket in Harlech.

Neither was enthralled by the prospect; it was just a weekly task that needed to be done. There was something happening though. Something happening in Glan-Y-Wern and if there was gossip that might follow, they wanted to be the ones in the know.

They shouted to Shelley to find out who the new people were and when she said they were reporters and that the Hunt's in Thistle-Do-Me were harbouring a known criminal, well they had to follow.

Lilly phoned Carol before they had gone ten yards and by the time they arrived at Thistle-Do-Me, there were villagers leaving their houses.

Next to Jessica, a man with what was clearly a television camera on his shoulder aimed it at Malory's face.

"Um, well it was our anniversary yesterday," she started to explain. Shelley, the unpleasant woman from the harbour who looked, dressed, and largely acted like a man, had already shouted over the top of everyone's heads demanding to know why neither Malory nor her husband had responded to any of her messages. Quite how Shelley got her number Malory had no idea, but she vowed to change it the first chance she got.

"We went out for dinner and a few drinks," Malory chose not to mention that ninety percent of the drinks went into her husband who then fell asleep before ... well, before he was able to be a husband. "And we got back late."

Jessica waited patiently for the bed and breakfast owner to continue, but made encouraging motions to keep her going.

"We, um ... we went to bed. It was late," Malory pointed out, hoping that might explain why they chose to retire. Next to her in their doorway, Joshua yawned. He had to be forced out of bed to make breakfast for their only guest this morning and was still moaning about the old vicar having vanished when the knock on their door came. "And this morning, like I said, he was gone. Actually though," Malory realised she hadn't answered the reporter's question at all, "he might not have been here last night. We didn't check. So, I don't know what time he left this morning or if he even came back here last night."

"There was bread missing," offered Joshua around another yawn. He had a headache and wanted to spend the day on the sofa staring at the TV. "Someone was in our fridge and there's a dirty plate with toast crumbs on it in the dishwasher."

Malory looked back at Jessica. "I guess he was here last night then. What is this about, please?"

"He's stinking rich," said Shelley, raising her voice so everyone would hear.

Jessica had been about to give Mrs Hunt a journalist's answer – something to the effect that they were investigating a story and then leave it at that since clearly the woman hadn't recognised Albert. Giving an answer went on hold though.

Spinning about to face the rough-edged harbour woman, Jessica asked, "What do you mean?"

"And his real name is Albert Smith," Shelley added, still talking to Malory.

Malory jolted, her brain connecting two dots that had until then been avoiding one another like opposite poles. Now, however, she saw it.

"Albert Smith! That man on the news! The terrorist! He's the man staying in my house!" She looked like she was about to faint.

Jessica wanted an answer from Shelley, but needed to correct Mrs Hunt first.

"Albert Smith is innocent. Have you not read the special edition of The Independent Enquirer? Or seen the news in the last few days."

Everyone was talking now; arguing about who knew what. The shocking news of a terrorist in their midst was the biggest talking point. People who watched the news knew there was an alternative theory being bandied about. It was breaking news though, so few had heard it and fewer had given it any credence.

Jessica had to battle her way through to Shelley who was happily the focus of many questions - locals recognised she knew more than anyone else and wanted to pick her brains.

"Well, it's kind of a secret," she revealed to Lilly and Carol who'd known Shelley since birth and could still be found having tea with her mum on occasion. Lowering her voice, she said, "He's won big on the horses."

Jessica's right eyebrow cocked itself. "Albert Smith won on the horses?" She wanted to say that he hadn't come across as a betting man, but had to admit she didn't exactly know him. Two days spent chasing criminals and getting shot at, plus a couple of hours in her car on the way to Cornwall hardly counted. Besides, as a journalist her job was to find the truth, not offer her opinion. "Can you be more specific?"

Shelley's mouth stopped halfway open when it rather abruptly occurred to her that she didn't actually know anything about the bet or even if it was horses he'd bet on. Recovering quickly, she tapped the side of her nose with one finger to show she was keeping the secret.

"The best person to talk to about that would be Curtis Jones."

Jessica's phone recorded the name. "And who is that?" she asked.

"Maud and Alf Jones's little boy," replied Lilly, stealing Shelley's thunder. "He's all grown up now, of course. He's the betting shop manager."

Jumping back in quickly, Shelley said, "Curtis said Albert Smith walked into the shop yesterday with the receipt from a bet he placed months ago in ..." she had to dredge her brain to find the name, "Melton Mowbray."

"Ooh, they make such lovely pork pies there," Carol felt the need to comment.

Pretending Carol hadn't spoken, Shelley said, "That's why we were here last night. I knew something was off with the old vicar when he had so many questions about the yacht."

"Yacht?" repeated Mike Atwell. He'd been listening quietly, always content to let people talk because they reveal so much when they do. "What sort of yacht?"

Shelley looked his way. "Oh, um, a big Sunseeker looking thing. Expensive. Belongs to the earl."

Mike, Oxford, Jessica and several more all repeated, "The earl?"

Shocked by the unexpected interest, Shelley almost took a step back. "Yeah, the earl. Earl Bacon. He owns, or his family owned most of the land around here. He sold his stately home to some foreign bloke a few years ago and vanished."

Mike Atwell remarked, "Albert was in Cornwall about a week ago. There was a gunfight on the quayside in Looe and a big search for a Sunseeker yacht seen leaving the area. The police didn't find it."

Jessica twisted to check her journalistic colleagues to find they were all furiously tapping on their phones to find more information. This was a new and exciting development. Was the earl connected to the Gastrothief in some way? Was it the same yacht that was in Looe? If it interested Albert, then it interested her.

Taking Shelley by the arm, Jessica said, "Which way to the betting shop, please? I need to know more about this money."

Somebody's Watching You

Two miles from the crowd now heading back down the hill into the village in search of Curtis Jones and the betting shop, Albert sucked on his teeth.

"There will be guards outside," he remarked. "Bound to be."

"Do you think they will be armed?" asked Asim.

Gloria nodded her head. "You can bet on it. Discretely though and that will work to our advantage."

Albert and his five companions plus Tabatha the cat were out of sight from anyone who might happen along the narrow coastal path. Having followed the gravadlax van this way yesterday, then losing Rex somewhere in this general area, to then be taken back here by the Gastrothief's agents, erased any doubt that the lair he hoped to find was here.

The only problem with that was the simple fact that there was nothing here. Nothing visible anyway.

The coastal path diverted from the main road just outside Glan-Y-Wern and traced the line of the cliff roughly fifty to one hundred yards inland all the way to Abergowd-Coed. There was not one single turn off. Or so they thought until Gloria pointed it out.

It wasn't a road. It didn't have tarmac, but between a line of trees at the leading edge of a thick copse and set at an angle to the road so it was hard to see and could easily be missed, sat a path just wide enough for a van.

Gloria, riding her motorcycle, saw it because she was looking for mud on the road where tyres deposited it when leaving the dirt path.

Now tucked fifty yards down that path, they were huddled to discuss strategy.

Gloria outlined her plan, checking with Albert to see if he would agree. She liked the retired detective, but he could be such an old woman when it came to taking risks with anyone else's life.

Albert scratched his chin. "I don't know. Sounds a little risky. What do you think, boys?"

Asim and Afshin were trying not to look worried.

Gloria spoke before they could. "They're ninjas, aren't they? This will be a walk in the park."

Afshin mumbled when he replied, "Well not exactly ninjas. We practice Tae Kwando and that's ..."

Gloria cut him off. "Potato, potarto. I'm going to ride up to the gate – there must be a gate or barrier of some kind. While I'm distracting whoever is there, you two sneak up behind and take them out. No shots get fired, no one has any idea what happened. Sound good?" she asked for the second or third time, immediately following her question by throwing her right leg over the seat of her bike. "Good. Let's go." She fired the engine to life and set off, leaving everyone else to figure out what they needed to do.

Asim said, "Um."

Albert placed a hand on his shoulder. "You don't have to do anything, chaps."

Toby puffed out his cheeks. "I don't know. That is one intense old lady. If she told me I needed to attack someone, I would probably do it."

Donna frowned at him. "You would get your butt kicked."

Toby laughed humourlessly. "Exactly. And I'd do it anyway because Gloria scares me more than a beating."

Afshin tapped his cousin's arm. "Come on, Bruv, let's get this done."

They jogged off down the dirt track with Albert reluctantly watching their departing backs.

Donna asked, "What do we do?"

They followed in the van, carefully easing down the track so they would see Gloria long before they came into sight of the barrier. Or so they hoped. As it turned out there was no barrier or guard hut, but they were in the right place.

"Hmmm," Gloria was off her motorcycle and harrumphing.

The dirt track ended with a piece of tarmacked road. It was two lanes wide and angled downward into the rock of the headland. Looking in the direction of the sea, the view was blocked by more trees, but Albert judged they could not be more than fifty yards from the cliffs.

The two lanes covered a distance of ten yards before they met a double height, double width steel door. There was no other visible opening.

Donna and Toby got out of the van to join Asim and Afshin who were staring at the giant steel obstacle.

"How the heck do we get through that?" asked Donna of no one in particular.

Albert replied, "*We* don't. *We* don't have to." Lifting an arm to point to the rock above the door, he said, "Those are cameras. They are watching us now. You should all get out of here. Get back to the village and raise the alarm."

Asim expressed his concern when he asked, "What are you going to do, Bruv?"

Albert pursed his lips and rolled his shoulders. "I'm going inside to see if I can reason with someone. The game is up. You will bring the police and from what you've shown me on the news today, it will take only minimal convincing to have them smash their way in here. This thing isn't on the map, and everyone knows I've been looking for a secret lair. I have to say," he chuckled to himself, "I never once really believed there would be an actual secret lair. Below ground to boot."

Gloria had wandered off back to her motorbike, which surprised Albert who thought she would be the first to argue against his suggestion.

"Will they hurt you?" asked Donna, her voice quiet.

Albert pursed his lips again, considering his answer.

"Probably," he admitted. "But I hope they will know there is nothing to be gained by killing me or anyone else. I believe there are people being held captive in there and I want to get them out alive. I want Rex back too and I'm willing to bet he is already inside."

Toby asked, "How?" but followed his question with a string of expletives when he saw what Gloria was carrying.

"My goodness this thing's heavy," she complained, resting the six-barrelled rotating minigun on the seat of her bike. "Stand back everyone. I'm going to take care of the cameras."

Inside the earl's underground bunker, a small crowd had gathered in the control room. They were not used to seeing anyone at the gate who was not supposed to be there. In fact it had happened only once in the history of the installation. That person, a rambler attempting to walk the entire coast of Great Britain, was invited inside at gunpoint and was still working as a janitor.

When the motorcycle and sidecar pulled up it did not cause a flurry of activity. The man in charge in the control room, Joel Watts, didn't even put down his mug of coffee. Acting calmly, like the seasoned veteran he knew himself to be, he dispatched two junior members of his team to collect the person outside.

However, before they could get down to the pedestrian access gate set into the main gate – they didn't want to open the whole thing until it was time to do so – two Asian kids appeared. Then an old man in a van with two more kids.

It was when he saw the old man that Joel put his coffee down. His hand missed the console for which it was aiming, the cup tipping and falling to smash on the floor where it splashed hot coffee across his boots.

When he saw what the old lady produced from inside her sidecar, he flipped open a clear plastic cover and slammed his palm on the big red button it hid. Throughout the biome, an alarm sounded.

Potential to Die

The pace of Argyll's pulse made him close to dizzy. He was about to attempt something that would either instantly result in his death or start him on a path that would either end with his escape or his death.

The potential for death was overwhelming.

When the alarm sounded, it cut through his nerves, spiking his heart rate even higher, but just ahead of him Tanya twisted to look back at the light shining out from the accommodation and he seized his chance.

Kicking out a leg at Ryan, Argyll planned to knock him down before driving a hammer blow at Tanya's head. They were still twenty yards from his smokehouse where he had planned to make his move, but an opportunity had to be grasped when it came.

With Tanya down, he could grab her gun and shoot Ryan. Risky, but like he already acknowledged, the potential for death was high.

His foot lanced backward toward Ryan's centre of mass. With all his force behind it, if it connected Ryan was going to fold in half.

It did not connect.

Ryan could see how twitchy the Scotsman was acting and was experienced enough to read his vibrating body for what it was: Argyll was charged up with adrenalin and waiting for the chance to try something stupid.

He almost missed it when the alarm sounded, Ryan's natural reaction to tear his eyes across to the main installation robbing him of a precious second. However, when the leg came arcing toward his gut, he was able to chop at it with a strong forearm, sweeping it around to throw his opponent off balance.

With Tanya's weapon raised to end Argyll's life, Ryan could have stepped back and let it happen. It would be messy though. Unnecessarily so. With a backhand swipe, he struck Argyll on the head with his gun.

The blow contained enough force to curtail any further stupidity on the Scotsman's part. Stepping back to give Argyll space to wince and bleed, Ryan said, "No one has to die today. You can live if you are bright enough to understand that you are beaten."

Argyll said nothing. The momentary stars that filled his vision were already fading. His head hurt and the skin on his forehead was cut. It wasn't bad, he knew, which is to say that it was bleeding but not gushing.

Left to struggle back to his feet, Tanya and Ryan motioned for him to go ahead and made it clear he would not live through a second such encounter.

At the smokehouse, he opened the door and stepped back to let Tanya enter first – they were not going to allow him the chance to grab something.

"He's in here?" Tanya asked, pointing her gun at Argyll's chest. It felt like a trap: there was no sign of the dog and few places a German Shepherd could hide.

Around a resigned sigh, Argyll motioned to the table. "There's a compartment behind there. The dog is inside it."

Ryan cocked an eyebrow. "A secret compartment. You had them strip and rebuild this place, didn't you. Very clever." His tone suggested he thought there was nothing clever about it at all.

Tanya made Argyll shift the table out of the way to expose the knee-high door it concealed.

"Open the door and stand back." She was going to shoot Rex the moment he showed his face. Not to kill; she already promised she wouldn't. The dog could manage with fewer than four legs though.

Missing Bet

At the betting shop in town, Curtis Jones was having a terrible time trying to explain why he couldn't find the betting slip Albert came in with the previous day.

"It was right here," he lied. It was in his wallet. His sure-fire, absolute get rich quick, one in a million opportunity was going up in smoke fast. Worse than that, he had pilfered the thing and if he got caught in his lie, would never be able to show his face in the village again. He'd lose his job too. And his wife would leave him.

Curtis Jones stared into the abyss of a bleak future, and it wore the unshakeable conviction of an investigative journalist. That she was backed by two men who introduced themselves as police officers, a camera crew, and more than a dozen of his fellow villagers did nothing to calm his rising terror.

The door opened as even more people he knew filed in. His shop was full to capacity, and it wasn't even opening time yet. He always came in early to do admin and only ever stayed past five o'clock if there was a big sporting event that would draw a glut of punters.

With a crowd outside hammering on his door because they could see him moving about in the back office, he felt forced to open just to see what they wanted. Now of course, he wished he'd kept the door closed and insisted they come back at noon when he officially opened.

Jessica knew well enough when someone was avoiding a straight or honest answer. Curtis was hiding something.

Pressing him to give up what he knew, she came from a new angle.

"How much has Albert Smith won?"

"I'm not permitted to divulge that information," Curtis replied confidently, feeling better to have a question he could answer honestly. "It will be down to Mr Smith to decide if he wants to reveal his winnings." Smiling for there was a camera in his face, he added, "I can, however, reveal that it is what many would consider to be a substantial amount." Thinking on his feet before the attractive redhead could hit him with another question, he aimed his face away from her, so he was looking straight at the lens. "Mr Smith placed an accumulator bet, one of Grand's Turf Accountants best chances to win big." As a statement it was true. It was also true that less than half of one percent of those using the bet ever won anything. Talking to an imaginary audience at home, Curtis went for his best gameshow host impression. Around a beaming smile he said, "Come down to your local Grand's outlet and win yourself a fortune."

The phrase just popped into his head and rolled off the tongue. He could see himself as the new face of the company. He continued grinning, the camera in his face and a bead of sweat trickling past his left ear. When two seconds passed and no one said anything, he cut his eyes to look at Jessica without moving his head or allowing his smile to fall.

She asked, "What are you doing?"

"We're live, right?" he sounded hopeful and doubtful at the same time.

Jessica rolled her eyes, not used to dealing with idiots.

Tapping Keith the cameraman on the arm, she said, "Might as well stop filming. I'm going to have a quick word with Mr Jones here." Taking hold of Curtis by an elbow, she aimed her head across the room. "Is that your office?"

Curtis managed to open his mouth, but no sound came out before he was being marched across the room.

"It'll do," Jessica remarked, steering the betting shop manager in that direction. "DS Atwell, would you and Constable Shaw be so kind as to wait outside the door so no one can get in, please?"

Jessica liked being bossy. It wasn't something new or forced, she had been like that since childhood. It played well with her career of choice and combined with her ability to read most people, and lie convincingly when she needed to, it made her a good investigator.

With the door shut and two the cops kind enough to do as she requested, she let go of Curtis' arm and was talking before he could turn to face her.

"The winning betting slip was here yesterday, right?"

Curtis had already admitted as much. "Yes."

"And you want me to believe that it has mysteriously vanished now?"

Curtis shrugged. He knew he wasn't getting the money now, that dream was gone. His lips were answering Jessica's questions, but inside his head he was desperately scrambling to find a new best scenario.

"Let me phrase it this way, Curtis. Either you or one of your employees has stolen Albert Smith's winning bet. I am going to leave your shop in just a few moments taking everyone with me. It just so happens that I know Robert Grand personally." She didn't. Jessica researched the company particulars on her way down the hill with Shelley jabbering in her ear. Curtis wasn't to know that though and Robert's address on Companies House was close enough to hers for it to be true.

She watched when Curtis's cheeks flushed with red and he swallowed hard.

"When we come back ... and we will come back ... I expect that missing betting slip to have magically reappeared." She came to Wales for the story of a lifetime. That there might be even more to it was beyond belief and she was going to wring every drop of truth from it. "Are you listening, Mr Jones?"

Curtis, feeling like he was being handed a lifeline, nodded his head vigorously. "Yes. I will get straight on it. If one of those …" He almost swore, but downscaled it before the word left his mouth, "toerags has taken it, even for safekeeping, I will have their guts for garters." At this point it occurred to Curtis that he could have said that was precisely what the betting slip was doing in his wallet. Too late now though, and he was still weighing up the odds of cashing it in on his way to the nearest airport.

Jessica watched Curtis for a few seconds more, sizing him up before acknowledging that she needed to move on. So far, she knew where Albert wasn't, but no one knew where he was.

The sound of sirens in the distance eliminated the desire to hang around any longer. There were police coming – it had to be the police – and that meant more story.

As the people vacated his place of business, Curtis made sure to lock the doors and slumped against the frame, his heart racing until they were out of sight.

It was still early in the morning, but did that give him plenty of time to enact a cunning plan, or too little because there would be nowhere for him to cash the winnings for hours yet?

Susie Dobbs and More

At the harbour, vacated less than twenty minutes ago by Jessica and her growing entourage, new people had gathered.

Among them was former PC Susie Dobbs. He'd travelled from Lancashire where he met Albert Smith and his dog just a few weeks ago. Albert had been there to taste the real Lancashire Hotpot recipe, but found himself embroiled in a TV show host's murder instead.

When Susie received the message from Albert late last night, he hadn't been able to figure out how to send it onwards with a motorcycle courier. This wasn't due to lack of funds or a problem with his brain, but because he was drunk.

His last day as a police officer came just eleven days before the message from Albert arrived. When he filed his decision to quit his time in law enforcement, HR made his transition very easy indeed. With anyone else they would have made them work their remaining time. In the case of PC Dobbs, they took his uniform the same day and wished him all the luck in the world.

He had a job in his uncle's bar less than an hour later. Susie Dobbs liked to drink and believed, wholeheartedly, that he was rather good at it. It was for that precise reason that he read Albert's message in a drunken blur and managed to delete it. A few hours later, awaking in a panic, the only part he could remember was that Albert, an old man who changed his life and made it oh so much better, needed his help.

Just about sober enough to drive, he found the name of the place he wanted after several attempts at remembering what it was called and set off.

However, now he was here in whatever the heck the place was called – Welsh names were so hard to pronounce – he didn't know what he was supposed to do.

When a police car with two constables came into sight, their sirens on because that's just fun to do, he aimed himself in their direction.

Constables Evans and Edwards killed the siren at the village outskirts, slowing from their *Fast and Furious* chase speed to cruise past the harbour. Dispatch wanted them to investigate a possible sighting of Albert Smith. They knew the name and the face from the wanted board at the station, but held not one shred of hope that he was here in deepest, darkest Wales. Why would he be?

The call was anonymous and thus most certainly a hoax. They didn't mind so much though; it gave them a nice drive out into the countryside, and they planned to get a cuppa somewhere while they 'made their enquiries' – code for wasting as much time as possible - before returning to base to confidently claim they asked about and found nothing.

When a chubby bloke stepped into the road ahead of their car waving his arms and calling for them to stop, Edwards almost crashed. He would have yelled for the fat idiot to get out of the way and threaten him with something tangibly enforceable, but the man had jogged to the driver's window and was waiting for them to open it.

"Sir, you just committed about seven different road safety violations," PC Edwards began.

"Yeah, I was a copper myself until last week, fellas," Dobbs shut Edwards up in an instant. "Are you fella's here to look for Albert Smith?"

Neither constable was expecting the question.

"Are you the one who made the call?" asked Evans.

A horn beeped behind their squad car and a van displaying the legend 'Montpelier – the Chocolate of Kings' went by in the other lane, the driver shouting something unprintable from his window.

"Let's get off the road, shall we?" Dobbs suggested.

In the carpark next to the harbour, which was busier now than the village had ever previously seen, Constables Evans and Edwards wanted to know what Dobbs knew about Albert Smith.

"I'm sorry," said a voice from behind them. They turned to see a woman in her early fifties. Slender and attractive with deep brown hair being tousled by the breeze and sparkling brown eyes like chestnuts in snow, she had a German Shepherd dog at her side. "I couldn't help but overhear you. I'm Jaqueline and this is Maggie. I got a message from Albert Smith last night. Are you all here to help him?"

Constable Edwards almost got to tell the woman it was his job to arrest Albert Smith when the sight of a small crowd caught his eye. They were coming out of a sideroad and heading directly for him. There was a woman at the front with dazzling orange hair and she had a man with a television camera right on her heels. The rest of the people might be locals, he judged, except for one or two who had the demeanour and bearing of police officers.

Something was going on. He would need to radio it in, but chose to wait until he had a clear picture of what to report.

Things a Lady Keeps to Hand

"**Y**ou might want to put your fingers in your ears." Gloria gave the advice but no time to perform the feat before she pulled the trigger.

The sound of six barrels spitting bullets at a rate of six thousand rounds per minute is not something a person can easily describe. Saying it was loud fails to give colour to the picture.

That she only held the trigger for four seconds and in that time created a pile of brass shells on the ground by her feet demonstrated the incredible firepower of the deadly weapon.

By the simple expedient of swivelling the gun from left to right and tilting it to change the angle of elevation, she was able to zero in quickly on the cameras, destroying each of those she could see in a heartbeat.

Cackling when she released the trigger and the minigun ceased firing but took a second or so to stop rotating, she grinned at Albert and his young friends.

"I've been looking for an excuse to use that ever since I got hold of it," she revealed while removing her earplugs.

Uncovering his ears, Albert asked, "Where the heck were you hiding it?"

Gloria widened her stance to improve her balance and hefted the giant gun up and across so she could lower it back into her sidecar.

"Underneath Chuckles," she replied.

Coming to stand beside Albert with his ears ringing and unable to believe his eyes, Asim said, "Who's Chuckles? Is that the name of her rocket launcher?"

Gloria answered for Albert. "I don't have a rocket launcher, thank you very much, young man. Chuckles is my snake." To prove her point, she lifted Chuckles' head where he was curled on the ground by her feet.

Asim said, "Waaaaah!"

Toby swore, apologised, swore again, and decided to shut his mouth.

Only Donna was unflustered by the presence of such a huge serpent. "Oh, look at him," she cooed. "He's gorgeous."

Chuckles winked at Tabatha who was backed into the far corner of her carrier hoping the thing that made all the noise was gone now and would never be back.

"You sssssee, Tabatha?" Chuckles sniggered. "Sssssnakessss are gorgeoussss."

Albert's attention was back on the giant steel door and the problem it presented. With the cameras knocked out the people inside could no longer see him. It was hardly an improvement and since he figured they would have seen Gloria and everyone else arriving, surely there was someone on their way out.

Gloria presented a solution. Fishing around in the items unpacked from her sidecar, she produced a toolbox. From it she took a thick line of what appeared to be cable. Using a pair of heavy-duty snips, she cut off a length about nine yards long. Together with a reel of cable that led to a small silver probe she had hooked into the crook of her left elbow, she set off for the door.

When Gloria passed Donna, the younger woman asked, "What's all that?"

Her question made Albert's eyes twitch to the right whereupon he almost choked.

"Dear, God, woman. You're not really going to ..."

"Got a better idea?" she threw her question over one shoulder, never breaking stride as she advanced on the door.

Albert started to back away. "Everyone, you might want to be somewhere else. Get to the trees at least." He hadn't seen detonation cord for years, but it was an unmistakable product. Designed by the military to be used to clear trees blocking routes or deny the enemy broken down tanks they might otherwise repair, it had a million uses in the commercial world.

Easy to shape, one simply laid it out, connected it to a cable and turned on an electrical supply. The explosion was instant.

Half a mile away, the nearest human being to the explosion, if one discounts those inside the bunker and those setting it off, had been watching a van displaying the livery of a Swiss chocolate company trundle along the coast road. It seemed very much out of place which made the man curious. The van turned off the road and vanished into a line of trees.

Sensing that he had just witnessed something extraordinary, Chief Inspector Ian Quinn eased the car into first gear and set off after the van.

Inside the bunker, the pair of security guards, junior ones and not very well trained unlike the veterans the earl hired to do his dirty work, were running to get to the door. Eager to impress, they were going to deal with the person outside - an old lady they were told. Just collect her and bring her in: simple instructions even they could follow.

They were ten yards from the pedestrian exit when it and a rough circle three times its size simply ceased to exist.

In the Smokehouse

Tanya's itchy trigger finger had grown bored of waiting for Rex to come out. It was quiet enough for her to know the dog was not in there, so turning her gun on Argyll, she decided she was going to shoot him instead.

The explosion at the front door sent a catastrophic wall of pressure into the earl's accommodation. Deep underground and with nowhere to go, it burst windows and blew doors clean off their hinges. It finally dissipated when it broached the doors into the cavern, shocking thugs and captives alike where they congregated still in the centre of the settlement.

A lance of flame from a ruptured gas line set a fire burning, bright orange flames licking up the inside of a room facing Zion before the reverberations from the explosion had even begun to settle.

Rex had been waiting for a time to charge. He went into the dark hole because Argyll asked him to, but he didn't like it and felt trapped again. Searching and probing, he found a loose stone in the side wall of the cubby hole and over a few minutes managed to force enough rocks aside to push his way out.

Circling the smokehouse, he went back inside to wait and knew well enough to hide when he heard Tanya outside.

He wanted the humans in the right position relative to where he hid. Actually, he wanted Tanya in the right position, but when the explosion rocked the very ground on which he laid and he let out a little involuntary yelp of fright, he knew the game was up. It was a case of strike now or strike never.

Bursting from his hiding place behind the fish splitter at the far end of the room, Rex leapt at the first human he came to. It wasn't Tanya, the one he wanted, but a man holding a gun.

Concerned about the alarm when it went off a minute earlier, Ryan was shocked by the explosion. Inside the smokehouse, he couldn't see the devastating effects the blast had on the installation, but he heard it.

Gripped by momentary fear, he got no chance to wrestle it under control. From the corner of his eye, he saw something coming for his face. That was all the warning he got.

Rex hit Ryan with every pound of muscle he possessed, rocking him back as he sunk his teeth into the man's arm.

Argyll had been just as shocked by the abruptness of the explosion, but he didn't question what it was. In many ways he'd been waiting for it: Albert Smith was here.

Swinging a mighty haymaker punch, he put everything he could into removing Tanya from the equation. Not normally a violent man, Argyll knew he could kill today ... might be forced to kill today, and was going to feel no remorse about it.

Tanya's years of training and countless hours spent in dojos, enabled her to block most of the Scotsman's fist. However, she thought he was aiming at her head, and he was not. The gun skittered from her hand when his rope-a-dope move caught her out and his other hand hit her right forearm hard enough that her hand went dead.

Beyond Argyll, she could see Ryan was losing to the dog. The giant German Shepherd had hold of his right bicep and was thrashing back and forth. Ryan screamed and swatted at the dog, but he was losing a lot of blood, most likely from his brachial artery.

Rex spat the arm out, his teeth bared at Tanya as he came to stand beside Argyll.

Tanya glanced to see where her gun had gone, couldn't spot it and chose to cut her losses. The dog had beaten her once already when it ran through her legs in Kent. She'd tried to blow it up and drown it, yet here it was coming for her again.

Rex growled and bunched his leg muscles ready to launch his next attack.

Tanya spun on her heels and ran, reaching into a pocket with her good hand.

Rex leapt forward, certain he could catch her before she made the door. He saw that she dropped something, her hand throwing it to smash in his path, but he paid it no mind. Until the scent slammed into his nose like a chemical attack.

Tanya shot through the door and kept running, checking over her shoulder only once to be sure she wasn't being followed.

Argyll ran to Rex's side. The dog was still on his feet, but clawing at his face with both front paws.

Unable to avoid the smell himself, Argyll asked, "Is that peppermint? She hit you with a mint bomb? Is that even a thing?"

Rex had no idea. He knew peppermint when he caught the scent, but this was pure mint extract and powerful enough to burn the inside of his nose. It was the canine equivalent of being attacked with pepper spray and his face hurt.

Argyll collected Tanya's handgun, then went to find Ryan's. Ryan was still on his back, frantically applying a tourniquet under his right armpit to slow the loss of blood.

"Help me," he begged. "I'll die without medical assistance."

Argyll just shook his head. "Too bad."

He turned back to see if Rex was able to leave only to find the dog was nowhere in sight. Rushing to the door, it took a moment, but he spotted him, the black and tan fur shimmering with motion as he ran. Ahead of him and nearly at a door leading into the accommodation – it was hanging open Argyll noted – Tanya was trying to escape.

Sucking in a deep breath for it was time to rescue everyone else, Argyll whispered a prayer and said, "Good hunting, Rex."

Hero Speech

In the harbour carpark, a heated discussion about who was in charge and what they were going to do next ended when the sound of an explosion whumped into the air. Like an unnatural roll of thunder, it hit the clouds and bounced back, the cracking rumbling noise echoing outward from its point of origin.

Everyone stopped talking.

Mike Atwell looked up at the sky then down to find Oxford looking at him with a grim expression.

Someone asked, "What the heck was that?" but Mike was already moving toward his car.

Jessica caught his arm. "That has to be Albert. What are you going to do?"

"You've got wheels, right?"

"Of course."

Mike held up a hand to stop her saying anything else. He was making a precarious decision and he knew it. Placing a hand on the bonnet of his car, he clambered onto it so he stood three feet above everyone else.

"Ladies and Gentlemen. Those of you who are here specifically because Albert Smith sent you a message and those of you who simply live in this corner of the world, there are people not far from here being held captive by a megalomaniac master criminal. That is what drew Albert Smith to this place. I'm willing to bet my pension the explosion you just heard was him breaking into the Gastrothief's secret hideout ..."

Jessica hissed, her voice quiet so the microphone wouldn't pick it up, "Tell me you are getting this, Keith."

He gave her a thumbs up but didn't move the camera.

"... I am going to the source of that explosion now. I am not armed, but I am imbued with the ability to place people under arrest. I intend to do that. To do whatever I can to make sure Albert Smith wins this day and the people he came here to rescue go free. You do not have to come with me, but if ever there was a time to be brave. If ever there was a time to stand up and do what is right, this is it, good people. Join me now and let's storm a madman's lair!" he finished with a shout and a fist punched into the air.

"And we get to be on TV!" shouted Dobbs which sealed the deal for more than half the gathering.

Feeling silly now with his fist in the air and no one applauding as he imagined they might, Mike Atwell jumped down from his car's bonnet and slid into the driver's seat. Before he could get the key in the ignition, Oxford was in the passenger's seat and Dobbs was piling into the back.

All around him once they saw others running for their cars, the rest of the crowd found someone who had a set of wheels nearby. Within seconds cars were tearing out of the carpark and turning left to blast up the hill out of the village.

They were guessing where they had to go, but with Shelley in the back of Mike's car wedged in next to Dobbs, they had a good idea.

Pointless Chivalry

The blast wave from the explosion went both into the cavern and outward from the door to bend the trees and fling dirt and leaf litter into the air. Albert, Gloria, and the kids were hugging the ground when she hit the button, but they got pelted anyway. Chuckles was underneath the sidecar and Tabatha was safe inside her carrier, but that didn't stop the explosion from putting the wind up them.

Squawking and complaining, Tabatha tore at the little door trapping her inside the protective carrier until it popped open. Bursting from her cage with a plan to run and keep running, Gloria caught her in mid-air.

Cooing and stroking, while the cat dug her claws deep into the leather of her motorcycle jacket, Gloria said, "There, there, Tabatha. Mummy has stopped making noise now. Sorry about all the fuss. Now we need to rescue some people. Can you help mummy with that?"

Gloria didn't understand her cat's reply which was for the best given the number of expletives it contained.

"You too, Chuckles," Gloria insisted. "Could you give me a hand, please, Albert?" She indicated the enormous and heavy boa constrictor.

"Oh, um, I'm not sure I can lift him."

"Well we can't leave him out here, Albert. He might wander off."

Donna volunteered, "I can help. Are we going inside now? Is that safe?"

Albert gave her an honest response. "No, probably not. I think it best if you stay out here. I'm going in to look for Rex, but the rest of you have already done enough. Call the police; we ought to have done that already, but call them now. Tell them everything and get them to come with all the guns they can muster. If I'm right, this place is a hornet's nest of armed thugs and we just hit it with a big stick."

Everyone was back on their feet. The steel door had a huge hole in it. Big enough to drive a car through though not wide enough at ground level so it was going to be foot access only.

Albert started forward and got two paces before he stopped: everyone else was moving with him.

"What did I just say?" he flared his eyes at the innocent faces looking his way. "You've risked enough. Stay out here and call the cavalry."

Carrying Tabatha, Gloria hadn't even stopped walking and was now several paces ahead of Albert.

"You can stop the chivalrous act, Albert. Us ladies are not impressed by it. I already called the police, anyway. Ten minutes ago when you were messing about trying to decide what to do. If we wait for them to get here, they'll seal the place off and we'll miss all the fun."

Toby said, "Erm, I'm okay with missing some of the fun."

Gloria reached the ruin of the thick steel door. "Stay here then, kid. I've never been in a master criminal's secret underground lair. I'd like to have a look around."

With that, she clambered through the hole still holding Tabatha to her chest, her voice echoing out from within, "Can somebody please bring my snake? Chuckles won't want to miss this."

Exhaling an exasperated breath, Albert said rude words in his head, but resigned himself to the company he was keeping.

"Anyone who's coming, now is the time." With a pause to work out which bit of the snake he was supposed to lift it by, he got a hand from Donna who convinced Toby he had to help whether he wanted to or not.

"It's just a snake, Toby," she belittled him. "It won't bite."

Eyeing it sceptically, he said, "Are you sure?"

He got a grin in return. "Positive. It's a constrictor."

Muttering under his breath about how that was hardly any better, Toby carried the boa's tail end and the trio passed through the portal and into the semi darkness beyond. With Asim and Afshin tagging along, they set off to see who or what there was to find.

This is it, Ian

When an explosion sent a shockwave through the trees to Chief Inspector Quinn's front, sending birds into the air and scattering detritus in every direction, it came as a shock, but only until he remembered he was tracking Albert Smith, the person he had originally blamed for the bomb on Whitstable Beach. How dearly would he love to be able to prove he'd been right all along?

The Swiss chocolate van shot back into sight, reversing at great speed onto the road without the driver once looking to see if it was clear. The driver slammed on his brakes, threw it into first gear and left rubber on the tarmac when he floored it to get away. It shot past Quinn's car heading back to Glan-Y-Wern with a determination that suggested it wasn't going to stop until it was in a different country.

Chief Inspector Quinn let it go. He was here for bigger fish.

"This is it, Ian," he shifted position to look himself in the eye using the rear-view mirror. "This is what will make you Chief Constable of Kent."

There was no one around. Not a car in sight now that the chocolate van had vanished over the horizon. In the aftermath of an explosion, he was duty bound to see if anyone needed assistance. There could be injured persons. Not that he really needed an excuse; no one was going to believe he was there by accident, and he would never claim that was the case.

When he got the chance, he would make sure the press found him and do his best to sound humble while he played down how he singlehandedly caught Albert Smith, the people helping him, and the people Albert Smith had correctly, yet misguidedly identified as criminals. It wasn't Albert Smith's job to conduct the investigation, a fact he planned to make clear to anyone who would listen.

Pulling up behind a white Ford Transit van, Ian Quinn nodded to himself. He had thought of everything; he was a superb tactician. That was how he came to be first on the scene. Like a grand master playing chess, his opponent, or in this case opponents, would have no idea they were out of luck until he moved the final piece (himself) into position.

Now all he needed was a little bit of luck.

Approaching cautiously, he came to a ruined steel door. The twisted, fractured nature of the metal made it quite clear it was the source of the explosion. Stepping inside, he withdrew his baton and kept it at the ready should he need to deploy it.

A few yards in he found two young men dressed in matching black clothes; trousers and a shirt – a uniform of sorts. They each had a holster for a weapon on their right hip but the weapons themselves were missing. Both men were unconscious and had small trickles of blood coming from their ears.

Quinn recognised the injuries as the effect of being too close to the explosion: concussion wounds. They would survive but their hearing might never be the same again.

Pushing onward, he heard what sounded like shooting in the distance; automatic weapons being discharged.

A Shot at Freedom

Argyll ran all the way back to the gaggle of houses that formed their captive community, only slowing when he drew near to where the residents were congregated – he didn't want the armed thugs to hear him coming.

He had two handguns, both with fully loaded magazines. He'd handled a shotgun in his life, that was nothing more than country living and useful to ensure there was grouse or rabbit for tea when money was a little thin on the ground. Handguns though, despite seeing hundreds of action movies, were something else.

He believed the safety catches were off, but until he tried to pull the triggers, he wasn't going to know if they would fire. It worried him to say the least.

Seven armed thugs came to Zion, two went with him and they were out of the equation now. That meant there were five he needed to ... kill. Argyll forced himself to acknowledge what needed to be done. He and his companions could escape. The doors to get into the accommodation were all hanging open. All they had to do was get past the guards.

Sidled up against a building, he took two deep breaths, raised the mismatched guns, and stepped into the open with his arms out ahead like arrows. He believed he could get at least two. At least. Surely Benny and everyone else would know this was their best shot at getting out. They would overcome their fear and tackle the armed thugs before they could get a shot off.

Expecting to find everything more or less as he had left it, Argyll was shocked to discover it was anything but.

Benny was holding a gun. So too were David Merchant and Neil McFadden. On the ground, three of the guards were tied up and gagged.

"Argyll!" blurted Christina, the first to spot him. All heads swung his way.

Lowering his guns, he had but one question. "What the heck happened?"

Benny stepped forward, proudly toting his gun like a trophy.

"There was an explosion. You probably heard it. Everyone flinched including this bunch." He poked one of the thugs with his boot. "Then two of them legged it and when the others turned to shout at them, we attacked."

One of the guards raged behind his gag and fought against his bonds. Benny kicked him in the hip.

"Well, what are you still doing here. We've got to go! This is our chance!"

"We know that, Argyll," snapped Christina, the tension getting the better of her. "People are grabbing their things."

"Things?" Argyll could scarcely believe people were stopping to collect their belongings.

"Yes," she snapped again. "Debbie thought it might be a good idea to get her kids."

"Oh, yeah, fair point."

"And Mitchell needed his insulin. He wasn't going to risk leaving without it. Wait," suddenly Christina was looking around Argyll. "Where's Sarah?"

Now Argyll was looking at everyone else and not just Christina. "What do you mean? I left her here."

Benny said, "She went after you."

"I'm here," Sarah arrived breathlessly back in the hub of the settlement just as Debbie appeared with her kids and Mitchell came from the other direction having fetched his meds.

"What do we do with these guys?" Benny toed the guard on the ground again causing a fresh set of muffled expletives.

Argyll didn't even need to think. "We leave them where they are. This is about us and about getting back to civilisation. Everyone grab a weapon if you can."

With iron garden tools, knives, and the few guns they'd taken from the guards, the captives of Zion made haste across the cavern floor to get to the earl's accommodation.

Powder Keg

Argyll and the other prisoners were not the only ones with escape on their minds. Joel Watts knew the gig was up and told everyone else to get out while they could. His instruction wasn't altruistic; Joel believed he stood a better chance of getting away if there was a whole bunch of them scattering to the four winds at the same time.

The installation was on fire. The fire suppression systems were fighting it and would win, but the damage was already heavy – Joel believed the underground bunker was doomed.

There being only one way in or out, he ran for the stairs. The team he left behind in the bunker looked at each other for a two count, then jumped to their feet as one and ran after their team leader. They converged at the door, all trying to squeeze through the bottleneck at the same time.

There were some naughty words employed and a boob got accidentally fondled, but they burst into the corridor beyond and ran hell for leather.

They got to the stairwell in record time but there they caught up with Joel who was unable to go any further.

The earl was blocking his path.

Pasty faced and sweating, the overweight member of the peerage had one hand clutching his chest and the other held at shoulder height, palm out to halt their progress.

"What do you mean you are abandoning the facility?" he demanded to know, his voice strained and his breath coming in short gasps.

Until that moment, Joel Watts had always addressed the earl as 'Sir'. With smoke drifting in the air and the alarm wailing above their heads, he ditched any thoughts of formality.

"Are you mad, you silly fat git? The installation is on fire! The front gate just exploded and there are people inside the accommodation. The police are coming, you mad fool!"

The earl took a deep breath, hoping to get some air into his lungs just so he could speak. The pain in his chest was becoming unbearable. Still blocking the exit route with his enormous girth, Earl Bacon screeched his thoughts, starting with, "How dare you! I am your employer and your master. I am directly related to the King of England! Moreover, this is the safest place on the planet even when it is on fire. You should be running toward the flames to put them out, not away from them. The world will end soon," the Earl shifted his gaze to look at the others impatiently waiting behind Joel Watts, "you all know this. The world is heading for a man-made cataclysm that cannot be avoided. Here you are safe. Here we can hide from the disaster outside. Now, back to work, all of you. Chop, chop." He took his hand away from his chest to clap both hands together. "Off you go."

Joel shoved by him with a sneer. "Stay here and die then. It looks like you already are. I'm getting out while I can."

Pushed back against the wall, Earl Bacon clawed at his employees when they rushed by, but he had not the speed nor the strength to stop them.

Watching them sprint down the stairs and out of sight, a fresh spike of pain stabbed at his heart. On wobbly feet, he turned the other way and started to shuffle back to his palatial quarters. A drink of something, that was what he needed. Yes.

One flight down, Joel met with a dozen other people all running in the same direction. Anyone working on this level was evacuating it. No one was staying. That was how it looked. It came as no surprise that all the earl's employees had reached the same conclusion.

The entire operation was all supposed to be super-secret. No one knew about the earl and his desire to hide from the world. Half the folk thought he was a crackpot, but he paid too well to let that bother them. The rest bought into his crazy story about the impending end of the world.

It wasn't enough to convince them to stay now though. They were under attack for a start, but the questions began two days ago when The Independent Enquirer broke their story about a mysterious criminal mastermind called the Gastrothief.

Somehow, there were people out in the world who knew all about the earl's hired thugs; the ones who went out to kidnap and steal and in many cases kill. In twenty-four hours it was all any of the earl's employees could talk about. The place became a powder keg. One that had actually just exploded.

Reaching the bottom level where they could race to the door and get outside, they encountered one of the intruders.

The man was tall and lean like an endurance athlete. With nary a flourish, he flicked out his right arm to extend a telescopic baton. His left hand came up to chest height and when it did, he began to speak in a loud and confident voice.

"Halt, all of you. You are all under arrest. I am Chief Inspector Quinn. There are police officers inside this facility. Surrender now or you will be taken by force."

Joel wasn't at the head of the charging mob running for the pinprick of light a hundred yards to their front, but he wasn't far back. He didn't stop when the lone police officer told him to and nor did anyone else.

The man with the baton swiped and swatted, the yowls of pain and curse words filling the air demonstrating that he managed to land a few blows. However, he was bowled over by the wave of stampeding humanity before Joel reached the spot where he'd taken his stand.

Joel's foot fetched up against a body on the floor – the cop had curled into a ball and was hugging himself, his head tucked against his chest – but he didn't stop, there was daylight ahead.

Priorities

Albert heard the sound of running footsteps as did the rest of his party. Asim darted back along the corridor they were in to take a look.

"Looks like people in uniform?" he reported, asking a question of Albert. "They're heading for the exit. Dozens of them."

Albert's sole purpose at this point was to rescue the captives. He was certain they were here. They had to be. It was going to be a disappointing day if they were not.

The Gastrothief, Tanya, the other people who had to work here for such a large underground facility to operate ... they were of no interest. At least, they were of no immediate interest. To properly clear his name, Albert knew he would need to present the police with someone new to arrest. That was going to be the earl. The Gastrothief. Albert would bet his pension the man behind it all was here somewhere. He still had no idea what the place was or why it existed, but it really didn't matter.

He was here to find Argyll and whoever else was being held.

And Rex.

Albert wasn't forgetting about Rex.

With fresh concern for his dog banging in his head, Albert threw caution to the wind to bellow his name.

"Rex!"

"Rex!"

The others joined in, Gloria, Donna, and everyone with Albert lending their voices.

After five seconds of shouting, Albert begged everyone hush so he could listen.

They couldn't know it, but they were on a heading perpendicular to the cavern. In ten yards they would face a choice to turn left or right. There they would find the broken doors leading out into the underground cave and the lights shining down over Zion.

They never got that far.

"Shhh," Albert stopped Asim just before he could speak. "I heard something."

Albert wasn't wrong. What he heard was his dog barking.

Worthy Adversaries

Rex's nose, the one sense he could rely on at all times, was playing up. The peppermint bomb had really messed with it. It felt singed, cauterised even. The insides burned like they had been rubbed with a hot chilli.

Any other dog would have whimpered and found a place to lie down. Rex was not like other dogs.

Sure his nose stung and his eyes were streaming; he used it as fire to make him madder than before.

At the police dog academy he was the best at the game of chase and bite. The handlers would don thickly padded suits and the trainees would chase them, biting hold of an offered limb to then wrestle the laughing human to the ground.

Rex rarely went for the padded bits. Why would he? Real criminals wouldn't be wearing them. In the real world, he'd played chase and bite many times and rarely failed to catch his target.

Tanya had eluded him too many times already. He rued not biting her in Kent when he had the chance. He ran through her legs instead to get to her partner. He would not make the same mistake today.

Tanya was going down.

Operating on maybe one tenth of its usual strength, his nose could still track her scent. It was easier than it would be anywhere else because they were in tight corridors where there was almost no breeze. The air ventilation system that swapped out the exhaled carbon dioxide failed when the explosion went off, so her scent hung on the air like a breadcrumb trail for him to follow.

Hot on her tail, Rex paused when he heard voices. Lifting his head and cocking it to one side, he listened.

The sound came again. It ... it sounded like his human.

Rex's tail gave a wag of excitement. Since falling through the vent almost a day ago, he'd been telling himself his human would find him if he just gave the old man enough time. Filled with happiness he could barely express, his tail stopped moving when he realised he couldn't tell which direction the noise was coming from.

Worse than that, he couldn't smell him.

The sound of his human's voice came again, a distant and desperate cry. It was joined by other voices, a cacophony of sound bouncing off the walls, ceilings, and floors of the installation.

Any direction could be the right one and not knowing which one to take made his decision easy: he continued to pursue Tanya.

Not so very far ahead of Rex, the petite assassin was on her way to the only other exit in the facility. She knew about it only because she went through the earl's private things while he slept one night.

Finding the blueprints, she hand drew a map and found her way to it. The tunnel covered just over a mile to exit in the cellar of the earl's former stately home.

The passageway linking the installation to the stately home had been used only twice in recent years. As a boy, Hubert Bacon would venture down into the dark tunnel leading to the giant underground cave to pretend he was Batman. His father forbade him from doing so, but that just made it all the more tempting. Until he fell and broke his arm when he was nine.

No one knew he was down there, and it took them six hours to find him. After that they sealed it off, the temporary wall built over the entrance only removed when the adult Hubert, now Earl Bacon, conceived his plan to build a place where he could hide from the ruination of the world.

The floor of the tunnel had been smoothed and lights added at intervals to just about scare away the darkness, but Earl Bacon had grown too large and unfit to consider walking its length. It was for emergency use only.

Since he moved into the installation, the passageway back to the house had only been used once.

By Tanya.

She chose to check where it went one night ... just in case.

This was her second trip.

There was money in her account, wired there regularly by the earl. All she had to do was get out and never look back. There would be another job working for someone else when she wanted it. That was for later though; Tanya felt she deserved some time off first.

The tunnel ran from behind the kitchens underground in an almost straight line. She was more than ninety percent of the way along it when she heard the dog behind her.

There was no need to look; she could tell what it was and hear the pace at which it was moving. Her backpack was full of clothes, cash she'd just stolen from the earl's private stash, her guns because she could hardly emerge at the other end with them on display, and her favourite stuffy, Mr Bear. He was in her crib the day she was born and went everywhere with her.

She dropped the lot without a second thought. Had she tried to get to her guns to shoot Rex, she would have discovered he was too close. By the time she got the buckles open and the weapons out, it would have been too late.

Running for her life proved the better option and she was no slouch. She could see the door. It was less than fifty yards away. Tanya didn't bother to breathe, she just ran.

Behind her and eating up the distance between them, Rex was also running at his top speed. His silky coat flowed with the movement of his muscles like he was being filmed for a shampoo commercial. Not that he appreciated what he looked like. His only thought was for Tanya, his eyes locked on the meat of her rump where he planned to sink his teeth.

With twenty yards to go, Tanya risked a look over her shoulder. What she saw sent a shard of ice through her heart and the image burned itself indelibly into her brain. The dog's lips were pulled back to show his teeth and she imagined Lord Baskerville must have felt just the same.

Rex snarled when his eyes locked momentarily with Tanya's. It was his undoing.

No longer looking where his feet were going, his leading paw caught a piece of the tunnel floor that continued to jut above the smooth surface. He tumbled, howling when he went head over teakettle and back onto his paws.

Immediately back in pursuit, he tried to close the remaining distance, but could see he wasn't going to get there in time.

Tanya slammed into the door, twisted the handle, and threw herself through it. Hitting carpet with her back on the other side, she kicked the door shut and pushed against it with both feet.

When Rex slammed into it a moment later, it held. It was made of solid oak and though it was designed to be opened from either side, there was no way for Rex to operate the handle above his head.

Spotting deadbolts at the top and bottom and thanking the Lord they had not been in place, Tanya slid first one then the other home.

She could hear the dog's angry barks, but they were muffled by the thick door.

Sucking in ragged recovery breaths, Tanya allowed herself more than a minute to bring her breathing and heartrate back under control. She had sworn bloody vengeance upon the dog and Albert Smith, but she was going to cut her losses and leave instead.

It didn't occur to her to list them as worthy adversaries but that was essentially what they had become. The old man and his dog had proven to be too tenacious, too determined, and too damned impossible to kill. Going after them again would just be foolish and she knew it.

Her backpack with all her things was gone. It contained her passport which was a nuisance, but she could get another easily enough. She had the contacts. The dog might already have gone, but she wasn't going to risk opening the door to check.

With plans of sunny beaches and lazy days filling her head, Tanya found the stairs and left the earl and all that occurred in his employ behind her.

On the other side of the cellar door, frustrated to the extreme, Rex was heading back the way he came. It was time to find his human.

The Posse

Joel Watts broke into the daylight, leaping athletically over the tortured steel of the main gate to leave the installation. Having made it this far, he believed the worst was over. It was a couple of miles to get to the nearest village but from there he could vanish, returning to his old life with no one the wiser.

He landed with both feet, his smile of success already failing.

A camera faced him, filming from ten yards away. Those who emerged ahead of him were already on the ground, face down and being watched over by ... cops. There were two lads in uniform and a bunch more besides who might or might not be police officers, but were tackling Joel's co-workers as each tried to flee.

Panicked, Joel attempted to take a step backward. Maybe he could hide out inside the installation for a while? Yes! He could disguise himself as one of the captives, the cooks and whatnots the earl had producing his food in the cavern. He could emerge later looking like one of them and then slip away.

The next person leaping through the hole in the door collided with Joel's back, shunting him forward to sprawl on the ground.

"Well volunteered, Sir," said DS Mike Atwell, placing a knee on Joel's back.

More of the earl's employees were pouring from the underground lair, stumbling from the increasingly smoky environment inside to find they were better off staying where they'd been.

As the senior officer at the scene, Mike had taken charge. Arriving first but with a squad car hot on his bumper and two dozen other cars racing to keep up, he invited the locals from Glan-Y-Wern to form a posse.

"A posse?" questioned Oxford, whispering at Mike's shoulder so no one else would hear. "Like in the Wild West?"

Mike nodded his head. "Just like that. A posse is merely the term for a body of people summoned by the sheriff to uphold the law. Today I am Sheriff Atwell."

Jessica's cameraman caught the whole thing and the cheer from the locals who were so worked up and excited by this point they probably would have whooped and hollered if Mike announced they were all going to jump off the cliff.

Not for the first time, Keith the cameraman murmured, "This is solid gold."

Five minutes after arriving, Mike counted forty-two detainees. More villagers had arrived to bolster the number of those fighting for good, among them some of the burly fisherman who arrived with rope. Further improving their numbers and their stance as a body to enforce the law, a host of wives from the local farms all brought shotguns.

Now trying to control an increasingly unruly crowd armed with deadly weapons, Mike was about to order everyone to clear their breeches and break the stocks when the two armed gunmen who fled Zion finally made it to the front gate.

They came through the ruined portal with submachine guns in their hands. Meeting more than three dozen shotgun barrels pointed at their faces proved enough to convince them surrender was their best option.

Disarmed and restrained, they were moved to one side where Constables Edwards and Evans were using some locals to keep the suspects in check. They were also liaising with dispatch in the nearby town of Harlech. The usual junior officer got replaced by the station's superintendent when it became clear a serious event was taking place – the report of an explosion came less than five minutes after a call from an anonymous lady stating she was about to blast her way into a secret master criminal's lair.

The call caused a few chuckles in the station until their phone lines erupted into chaos.

The superintendent wanted to know precisely what was going on and continued to demand to speak with DS Atwell. Mike refused, leaving the two young cops to manage their boss.

When the flurry of people leaving the underground base dwindled to nothing, Mike weighed up his options.

Dobbs came to his side. "You think Albert is in there?"

Mike nodded. "Yup. That would be my guess."

"You think he might be hurt?"

"Only one way to find out."

He turned to see who was touching his arm.

"Hello," said Jaqueline. "I'm Jaqueline. This is Maggie." She indicated her dog who gave a bored wag of her tail; she'd seen it all before.

Mike's lips parted and stopped, a snippet of memory delivering a message.

"Maggie? As in the Maggie in Albert's message?"

"I believe so, yes. It would appear he sent the same message to a lot of people. Did I hear you say you were going inside to look for Albert? Maggie is an expert sniffer dog."

"So am I!" boasted a small dachshund, arriving next to Maggie with his tail wagging madly. "I know Rex! I can find him."

Maggie looked down at the sausage shaped dog. "There's no need to get excited, pup. We can search together if you like."

Above them more introductions were being done. Yet another person had received Albert's cry for help and had found her way to Wales. Arriving a few minutes earlier, Kate Harris, her brother Victor in tow, followed the line of cars as they raced up the hill and out of the village of Glan-Y-Wern.

She was glad she did for she was clearly now in the right place.

"Are we going in?" Kate asked.

With the sound of many, many sirens in the distance, Mike looked around and accepted that his work outside was done. Since Albert wasn't here, he had to be somewhere inside.

.

Reunited

Deep inside the tunnel of the Gastrothief's lair, Albert was hugging a wall. People were coming. Lots of them.

They weren't even trying to be stealthy in their movements which set him on edge. His shouts for Rex must have given away their location and now he and his friends were trapped. Asim and Afshin were poised in fighting stances ready to throw arms and legs the moment the first person rounded the corner. Gloria had produced a matched pair of knuckle dusters from somewhere and had her hands up ready for a fight. Chuckles had been hoisted into the air so he could wind himself around a light fitting ready to drop and Tabatha the cat ... well Tabatha was off to one side licking a paw to clean an ear. She had elected to not take part.

With Toby and Donna beside him, Albert told himself to be ready for whatever came around the bend.

The approaching footsteps were running, the sound on the steel walkway allowing Albert's group to countdown to the moment they would need to spring their ambush.

Three.

Two.

One.

"Waaachaaaaar!" Asim leapt into the air, his right leg arcing up to then scythe down.

Albert shouted, "No, stop!"

The first person into sight had a machine pistol in his right hand. The second person was a woman whose hand he held. The third person was Argyll.

Their slightly grubby clothing and the unshaven, dishevelled hair instantly gave away the fact that Albert was looking at the very people he came here to find. Seeing Argyll was the clincher.

"Albert!" The Scotsman pushed past Benny to get to the old man. "I knew you would come. I told them and I told them."

Benny clapped Argyll on the shoulder. "Yes, you did."

More and more of the Gastrothief's captives were filtering into the same space Albert and his friends occupied.

Seeing the people with Albert, Argyll offered his hand to shake. "I see you brought friends."

Albert smiled, but asked, "I don't suppose you've seen my dog, have you?"

Argyll was about to exclaim that he had and tell Albert how Rex had saved him and how he knew to be ready because Rex came and found him. He didn't say any of those things though. Instead he pointed.

"He's right there!"

Albert spun around so hard he almost put his back out. Bounding along the passageway to get to him, his bright-eyed, beautiful dog looked as happy as any hound ever had.

He dropped to one knee, opening his arms for Rex to come.

Rex never thought to slow his pace. The underground place was a maze of tunnels and only by retracing his own scent had he been able to find his way back. Now his human was here and everything was wonderful.

Knocking the old man over in his excitement, Rex danced and wagged his tail and licked Albert's face.

It was a Kodak moment, but everyone knew it was not the time to be hanging around. There was smoke in the air coming from a fire somewhere and the alarm continued to sound. More than that though, the captives just needed to get out. Some of them hadn't seen real daylight in more than a year.

"Come on, lad. Come on," Albert coaxed Rex to settle down and used his dog as an anchor to get back to his feet. "It's time we all got out of here."

There was much murmuring of agreement and then a scream of terror when Chuckles lost his grip and landed on Asim.

Salvaging Something Worthwhile

C hief Inspector Quinn had a busted lip and a black eye. None of his injuries were caused maliciously; they occurred when he attempted to stand his ground in the face of a panicked mob. His baton was ... well, he couldn't find it, so it was somewhere.

Walking with a slight limp, he saw people coming through the ruined steel gate behind him and stopped to listen.

There were dogs leading the way; Quinn could see two canine outlines silhouetted against the brighter light outside. He almost called out to them, intending to bring them his way so he could question who they were when he recognised Detective Sergeant Mike Atwell's voice.

He'd made it this far then. Perhaps something worthwhile could still be salvaged from the mess. It might not be much, it certainly wasn't worth the amount of effort and time, but catching DS Atwell in the act of helping a fugitive would be a small reward and that was better than no reward at all.

Planning to tuck himself out of the way until Mike's group had passed to then follow so he could observe his former sergeant in the act, Quinn's ears heard more voices. Stepping into a shadow, he watched Albert Smith and his dog come into view. He was surrounded by people. Dozens of them.

Quinn was stunned to observe what could only be the captives Albert claimed were being held. The old man hadn't known where or by whom, but he'd been right, nevertheless. Quinn wanted to make his move, to arrest Albert Smith since the warrant for his arrest was yet to be rescinded. There were too many people with him though. Vulnerable people. He would look bad if he did anything to impede their escape.

His feet twitched. Could he announce himself and be the one who brought the captives into the light alongside Albert Smith - he was the representation of authority.

Too late, Quinn saw his chance evaporate. Albert had seen Mike Atwell and vice versa.

One Last Task

Albert made a choking sound of surprise and joy. Walking toward him were people he'd never imagined he would see again. Kate and Victor Harris from Biggleswade, Jaqueline from Keswick, Oxford from Stilton. He was struggling to believe what his eyes were telling him.

Rex couldn't stop his tail from wagging. His malfunctioning nose would have detected their presence any other time, but none of that mattered because his friends were here. Hans the dachshund and Maggie the German Shepherd were straining at their leads to get to him.

As the gap between the two groups closed, Rex looked around to see if Rosita the saucy Afghan Hound from Arbroath was also with them. Disappointingly she wasn't, but the groups met and as the humans shook hands and kissed and hugged, the dogs wound their leads around everyone's legs in their own dance of greeting joy.

Albert had tears on his cheeks to see so many people he knew, and it struck him how lonely the last couple of weeks had been. Almost since he left Blackpool, he'd been on the run and in the thick of it. Now he could finally relax.

Or could he?

Thanking people and shaking hands stopped the progress of the captives momentarily. They paused to wait for Albert and for Argyll who was sticking by the old man's side. The former residents of Zion acknowledged their freedom was at Albert Smith's hands, but they could only wait for so long.

With the camera on them and Jessica asking questions, 'Who are you? How long have you been here? Where did you come from? What is your story?' they grew quickly impatient. They might believe their rescue was at hand, but they were still inside their prison. Daylight beckoned.

Seeing the captives were moving once more, Albert took a faltering step to follow.

"What is it, Albert?" asked Oxford. "Are you all right? Do you need a rest."

Albert waved his concerns away. "I'm fine. I'm fine. It's just …" Albert shuffled his weary body around to look back into the depths of the underground base. "Well …"

Jessica finished his sentence. "The Gastrothief. You're wondering about the Gastrothief, aren't you?"

Albert nodded, his eyes still staring into the facility, not out at the door and the people outside.

"I don't suppose …"

"He already left?" asked Mike. "No, Albert, we don't think so."

Jessica said, "The man you have been chasing is Earl Hubert Bacon. You asked Shelley Rankin, the lady at the harbour about a yacht. She said she wouldn't give you the information you wanted."

"But she told you," Albert guessed what Jessica was about to say.

She nodded. "He's not among those outside."

Albert drew a deep, deliberate breath through his nose, held it for two seconds, then exhaled just as slowly.

"I believe I need to wrap this little caper up once and for all."

He was about to start moving when a hand hooked into the crook of his left elbow. Albert turned to find Gloria leaning in close. "I'm going to make myself scarce, Albert." She dropped her grip on his arm. "The dust will quickly settle and when it does someone will think to ask where the explosives came from and how it is that the cameras outside came to be shot to pieces."

Albert opened his arms and pulled her into a hug.

"How can I ever repay you?"

Gloria sniggered. "Oh, I think you'll get the chance, Albert. Something tells me you have adventures in you yet."

He let Gloria go, the elderly woman recruiting two of the former residents of Zion to help carry Chuckles.

"Come along, Rex." With a click of his tongue and a little tug on the lead, Albert got Rex moving in the right direction. He left so abruptly the gaggle of people he was with got left behind and had to catch up.

Jessica dispatched two of her crew to film the captives as they went outside. They only had one camera with them, and Keith was going with her. The others would have to use their phones as best they could. It would have a 'found footage' vibe to it but that would only make it seem even more real.

When they reached a set of stairs and proceeded to climb them, a figure stepped out of the shadows behind them and began to follow.

Seniority

There were no labels on the doors they came to. Nor on the stairwells to tell them what they might find on each of the three levels. They didn't need them though because Argyll was with them.

Initially, he drifted toward the exit and daylight along with all the other captives. However, when he saw Albert fail to follow, he doubled back, taking Sarah with him simply because he was holding her hand and planned to never let it go.

Sarah was one of those who had met the Gastrothief. He'd had questions for her, and a stern warning should she refuse to bake the cakes that made her cottage bakery in Yorkshire so famous. The earl's quarters were on the third floor at the top of the installation where he had views down over the fields and the freshwater river, over the livestock and the sea pool.

Albert's pace slowed halfway between floors one and two and he muttered under his breath about people and their need for stairs. Why couldn't the Gastrothief live on the ground floor?

No one rushed ahead – this was Albert's show, and they would go at his pace.

Reaching the top landing finally, Albert needed a breather and a sit down plus a nice cup of tea and possibly some biscuits or a slice of cake. Telling himself that would come later,

Albert continued walking. Dobbs was holding the door for him to go through and both Oxford and Mike Atwell had gone ahead to check the area ahead was safe.

The floor changed from steel plate to thick rich carpet the moment one crossed the threshold and all around the furniture and fittings were those one might expect in a palace.

It was spotlessly clean and almost completely silent.

Almost.

The soft sound of someone sobbing floated out from one of the adjoining rooms.

Albert's group spared no energy on speculation. What they did do was fall in line behind him when he clicked his tongue at Rex and told him to 'seek'.

Rex sniffed the air. His nose didn't need to be operating at full capacity for this task.

Maggie came alongside him, and Hans pulled up by Rex's front paws.

Maggie sniffed too, and said, "You can lead, Rex."

Going slow for he could tell when his human was feeling tired or weary, Rex led him across the room and through a door. Albert's entourage of friends new and old, people he'd met on his journey around Great Britain filed into a dining room where a feast was set out upon a long table.

It was set with just one chair at the far end. In it, a man sat staring forlornly at the food to his front. Detecting the presence of new people, he looked up.

"I can't eat it," he moaned softly, rubbing his chest and wincing. "I think I'm having a heart attack. Can you help me?"

Keith the cameraman got himself into position with a clear shot of the man behind it all. Jessica compared the man she could see with the picture she had for Earl Hubert Bacon. It was him all right. The photograph was four years old, taken at the last royal event he attended before vanishing from public life. He hadn't changed much except perhaps to gain another chin.

Donna and Toby from Melton Mowbray, Asim and his cousin Afshin from Bakewell, Jaqueline from Keswick, the Harris's and Hans the dachshund from Biggleswade, Oxford Shaw from Stilton, Mike Atwell, Argyll, and everyone else remained quiet, waiting patiently for Albert to speak.

In his head Albert had imagined this moment many times. The things he might say, the actions he might take. In every version his words would be filled with vitriol and justified damnation. Now though, staring at the pathetic creature clawing at his chest, he felt pity and disgust.

There were no words he wanted to use, nothing he had to say.

"Please," the fat man at the end of the table begged. "I need my doctor."

Albert nodded to Mike Atwell. "Sergeant, this man needs to be arrested, but you should probably call a doctor first."

Mike nodded and turned to Constable Oxford Shaw. "Oxford, I believe this ought to be your collar. I'll gain nothing by it and Dobbs here left the service more than a week ago. Get your name in the headlines, kid. I'll sort out some paramedics."

Mike turned to leave and found himself confronted by Chief Inspector Quinn.

"Not so fast, Sergeant Atwell. You're under arrest. This man," he pointed an accusing finger at Albert, "is still wanted for questioning."

Rex snarled in warning, causing Albert to shorten his dog's lead. Truly, he wanted to let Rex bite the man but no good would come of it.

Quinn shot a contemptuous look at the dogs all glaring his way and continued to berate Mike Atwell, "You are still legally a police officer. Therefore you are technically breaking the law by failing to arrest him." Spinning to glare at Oxford, Quinn continued, "And did I just hear that you are also a police officer? Then the same goes for you. You are both under arrest."

"Wait a moment," protested Jessica.

Quinn roared, "I will arrest the rest of you for obstruction of justice." More calmly, he said, "Now, since I am not only the senior police officer here but also the only one not currently under arrest, I shall take both Albert Smith and Earl Bacon into custody."

From the doorway, a new voice said, "Oh, no, I don't think you will."

The Arrest

A lbert jolted to hear the sound of such a familiar voice.

"Gary!" he threw his arms out to pull his son into a hug. "Gary, my boy. Oh, my goodness it's so good to see you!"

Gary held his father and did nothing to stop the tears falling. When he broke the hug a few seconds later, he asked, "Are you okay, dad? Are you hurt?"

Albert's heart was beating as strongly as it ever had, and he felt like dancing. His eldest son was here.

"Never mind me, Son, I'm fine. Where are Selina and Randall? What took you so long anyway?"

Gary laughed as he wiped away his tears.

"They are coordinating things outside. It's been a bit of a busy day."

"Excuse me," Quinn interrupted. "Detective Superintendent Smith, I presume. Albert Smith's eldest child. I see the family resemblance. You are suspended from duty, are you not? Therefore you have no authority here. That leaves me in charge, so step aside and keep quiet while I carry out my duties or I shall arrest you too."

A grin spread across Gary's face. "Wow. Selina said you were an obnoxious pain in the butt, but I see now she was being generous. My suspension was rescinded this morning as was the warrant for my father's arrest." He placed a hand on Albert's shoulder to tell him, "That's why it's taken me so long to get here, Dad. I went back to work, showed them your message, and kicked off until they put me in charge of the investigation." Gary swung his eyes across to look at Jessica. "I have you to thank ... *we* all have you to thank. Breaking the story the way you did, telling it all and throwing everything people thought they knew into question ... it changed everything in an instant."

"So you're in charge of the Gastrothief case?" Albert confirmed.

"As of about four hours ago, yes."

"And you couldn't send anyone to help me any sooner?" Albert was half joking and half not.

Gary sniggered anyway. "Remember how you are always telling me that you don't need help and I should just let you get on with it?"

Albert didn't have a come back for that one.

Still unable to wipe the triumphant grin from his face, Gary explained, "I needed a helicopter to get here this quickly. I'm sorry to see I missed all the action though."

Gary laughed a little harder and everyone in the room was laughing too. Well, almost everyone. There was one person with his arms folded and an expression most could only achieve with a bowl of cold jelly in their underwear.

Seeing him standing there, Gary wiped the smile from his own face. "You can consider yourself dismissed, Chief Inspector. I'm sure you can find your way out. I'll be generous enough to leave you out of my report."

If Quinn had anything to say, it was cut off by the earl. He hadn't been ignored during the last few minutes of conversation, Jaqueline and Kate had been doing their best to comfort him until the paramedics arrived. They wanted to push his chair back but found that impossible – it would take a forklift to move it with his weight driving the chair's feet into the floor. So with some help they moved the table instead.

Just when Quinn might have chosen to spit a parting retort, Earl Bacon selected that moment to ... shall we say, 'vent to atmosphere'?

A belch emanating from somewhere deep inside his gut burst from his mouth while at the same time something not too dissimilar was happening at the other end. It seemed to go on forever, though it was probably no more than a few seconds.

Both women ran back to the foot of the table where everyone else watched and listened in horror.

When the expulsion of gas finally subsided, the earl smacked his chops together a couple of times and pressed a pudgy hand to his chest.

"Do you know? I feel much better now." Quick as a flash (in his own head at least) the man the nation knew as the Gastrothief jumped to his feet and ran for the door behind him.

He had a secret way out if he could only get there.

Watching the fat man lumber to the door at a snail's pace, Detective Superintendent Gary Smith said, "Constable Shaw, isn't it?"

Oxford's cheeks tinged with heat at being addressed directly by such a senior officer.

"Yes, Sir."

"Would you kindly arrest that man?"

Aftermath

The paramedics came to check the earl anyway who by then had a circle of officers from the local constabulary surrounding him. Cuffs would not go around his wrists, so while they waited for someone to find something bigger, they kept him in place using numbers.

Albert watched the arrest, but with that task complete, a bone-deep weariness crept over him. Sleep had been a rare commodity in recent days, and he'd eaten far too little. If nothing else, he knew he deserved to eat and drink whatever he wanted tonight.

Gary offered a steadying hand to help him clamber over the ruins of the outer gate – the police were in the control room, but it was so badly damaged by Gloria's explosives they couldn't get it open. Arriving back in the cool air outside, Albert heard someone start to clap. In an instant it was a handful of people. A second later it was a hundred people and those who weren't clapping were saluting him.

It was a standing ovation.

Gary stepped away from his father so there could be no one else in the limelight. Overwhelmed, Albert looked along the line of people cheering and applauding. His youngest son, Randall, and daughter, Selina were among those applauding. The former captives were there, gathered in clumps, locals from the village and the friends he'd met along the way. His eyes stopped suddenly when they picked George Benjamin-Mackie from the crowd. George stopped clapping to give Albert a wave and a thumbs up.

It was a moment Albert would never forget, but with the applause echoing off the rocks and trees, he knew the success they wanted to acknowledge was not his alone. With a crack from each knee, Albert lowered himself to kneel next to Rex's front paws.

"This is for you too, Rex," Albert had to fight to stop his voice from cracking. "I didn't do this alone and I need you to know that I know that." He pulled Rex into a hug and held him there. With his head against his dog's ear, he said, "I sometimes wonder if maybe it was you finding the clues and solving the crimes. Casting my mind back over the last few months, I know for certain I wouldn't still be here if it wasn't for you."

Rex turned his head to lick Albert's ear and said, "Atta boy."

A short time later, Albert had a half-drunk mug of tea in his hands and a comfortable seat in the back of a squad car when Jessica rushed over to him.

"Albert, I just remembered!"

Rex lifted his head from Albert's lap where he'd been dozing.

Albert had no idea what Jessica was about to reveal so said, "What?"

"You won on the horses! In all the excitement of finding the Gastrothief's lair and rescuing all those people, I'd clean forgotten about it."

Albert laughed at himself. "You know what? So had I. Hold on. What do you mean I won? I won what?"

"You don't know?" Jessica's voice was raised enough in exclamation that the people around her all took an interest.

"What's going on?" asked Selina.

"Your dad won big on the horses."

Albert moved Rex's head off his lap and swung his legs out of the car. "You just said I had won. You never said I had won big. What does 'big' mean, exactly?"

Generosity

At roughly the same time that Albert Smith and his friends were entering the Gastrothief's lair, Curtis Jones was leaving his betting shop and his old life behind forever. He had the receipt for the winning bet in his wallet and a vague plan to be drinking cocktails in Bermuda by the time the sun set the next day.

Halfway through his door, a Rolls Royce pulled up at the curb. Curtis had one arm in his jacket and stopped that way, frozen while he stared through the glass to see who it might be.

A plump woman in her late forties with glasses and short hair got out of the passenger side of the car. She took a moment to straighten her jacket, smoothing the creases from it until the back door on her side opened and a man got out.

Curtis had to catch his gum before it fell out of his mouth.

Robert Grand was here. The owner of the nation's biggest betting franchise was outside his shop.

Two hours later, it was just after noon, and he was supposed to be open. Instead, the doors to the business remained resolutely closed and he was sitting in his private office listening to Marissa Cardheart go over the plan for the umpteenth time.

The delay in getting answers to him yesterday was all to do with the name: Albert Smith. As Curtis now knew, it was the name of a wanted man and there had been some ethical discussions about what the firm ought to do given the circumstances.

Robert had reached out to a golfing buddy who just happened to be Commissioner of the Police of the Metropolis, the head of all police in London and pretty much the highest-ranking cop in the country.

The advice was to wait because there were developments following the lengthy article published two days ago (now three) by The Independent Enquirer. That changed a few hours ago.

Albert Smith was now not only considered to be innocent, but was likely to become a national treasure. Given what he had done, knighthoods and a mention in the New Year's Honours list were to be expected.

For Grand's Turf Accountancy the opportunity for positive coverage could not be over-stated.

Curtis had to fake going to a filing cabinet to get the ticket and pray no one was looking when he took out his wallet and made the betting slip magically appear from the drawer in which he had his hands. He both cursed his luck for not leaving sooner, and thanked the Lord that he hadn't. Sneaking off with a fortune when it belonged to a criminal heading for jail was one thing. Stealing from a folk hero, well that was another thing entirely.

Marissa and Mr Grand expected Curtis to know precisely where to find Albert Smith but accepted his response when he told them about the earlier visit from Jessica Fletcher and her entourage. They missed the explosion and the excitement that followed, only finding out about it when the first of Curtis's employees wandered in fifteen minutes late.

"How do you not know?" Russel had to ask. "It's all anyone is talking about. Half the cops in Wales drove through here this morning."

The delay worked to their advantage – Marissa had cameras of her own arranged to meet them at the shop. They would do a proper formal presentation at a later date in London because the shop in Glan-Y-Wern failed to represent the firm adequately. It was tired and had some of their oldest machines. However, they had guessed right, and the Albert Smith story was about to break. Coverage *now* was what they needed if they were to capitalise on the sudden interest.

With everything in place, all they needed was the man of the hour. Fortunately for them, and quite unexpectedly, they didn't have to go looking.

Gary Smith drove his father to the betting shop, parking his car directly behind a Rolls Royce. More cars parked behind him; Albert's friends, his other children, interested parties, the villagers who had been at the Gastrothief's lair ...

Jessica and her film crew were there too. They'd had to send one of their team to scare up more batteries for the camera and knew they had a mammoth task ahead to edit the footage. The documentary to come would be ground-breaking ... earth-shattering even, and the surprise ending to come was a bonus no one could have predicted.

Albert had Rex off the lead, the German Shepherd excited and playful at his human's side and unlikely to stray. Not even a squirrel widdling on his water bowl would take him from Albert's side.

"Where are we going?" asked Rex. "Is there anything to eat? Oh, weren't we here yesterday?"

Robert Grand opened the door to the shop and stepped into the threshold so he filled the frame.

"Welcome one and all to Grand's Turf Accountants. I am Robert Grand, owner of this fine betting establishment, and I believe I have the honour of meeting Mr Albert Smith." He extended his right hand, grasping Albert's and using his left to keep it in place when he turned to face Marissa's official cameraman.

Albert remained polite and gentlemanly, posing for pictures, but was thankful that it wasn't long before he was inside and they wanted to get down to business.

"Two point seven." Robert Grand repeated his previous answer.

Someone near the back of the room swore and more than one let out a low whistle of appreciation.

"Actually, the exact figure is two million, seven hundred thousand five hundred and twenty seven pounds and eighteen pence."

Albert merely nodded.

"What will you do with the winnings?" asked Marissa. She had a bunch of suggestions lined up, not least of which was placing more bets.

Other people might have needed time to think, but for Albert the answer came easily. Idly scratching the fur around Rex's neck as he sat comfortably in a chair opposite the owner of the betting firm, he gave it all away.

"I will be setting up a fund to help those affected by the Gastrothief ... Earl Bacon's criminal activities. The people who were set free today," he was very deliberate to not say 'who I set free', "have lost income and will need to pick up the pieces of their lives. The Porkers Sausage Factory in Reculver was burnt to the ground, equipment was stolen from I don't know how many different places. The money won't be nearly enough, but it will be a start. I'll be looking for someone to manage the fund and review each case. I need to put some more thought to it all, obviously, but that's what I am going to do with it."

"Not going to keep anything for yourself?" Marissa could feel all her PR opportunities slipping through her fingers. She wanted to follow up the campaign about Albert Smith winning with pictures of him sipping cocktails in the Caribbean, or driving a sportscar through Monaco. What could she do with a charity fund?

The matter settled so far as he was concerned and the money due to be transferred to his bank account, Albert announced that he needed to buy people a drink. There was much argument, but he raised his voice to insist.

"Most of you came here to help me. You didn't have to, and you did it at your own expense. There's nowhere for you to stay here." He chuckled to himself. "I'm not sure I have anywhere to stay myself and that's the point really. Whatever happens next, you will all go your separate ways, heading back to those places where I first found you. To the people who dropped everything and travelled here when I inadvertently called for your help, I will never be fully able to express my gratitude. To the wonderful people of this lovely locale, I thank you from the bottom of my heart for rallying to my cause this day."

There was more cheering and more tears and both things continued for several hours at the Old Seamaster where Glynn Travis could once again not believe his luck.

On the Way Home

In the morning, Albert awoke with daybreak and took Rex for a walk down to the harbour and back. The temperature had dropped; a cold front had moved in from the north and later that day he saw an odd news report about a snow beast leaving footprints in Rochester High Street.

Back at the bed and breakfast, he ate a sumptuous full English and fed Rex sausages from his plate. His children arrived just after nine – they'd found rooms for the night in nearby Harlech.

"Are you ready, Dad?" Selina asked after giving him a quick hug. They were all trying not to make a fuss, but they really wanted him home now so they knew where he was.

Albert pursed his lips and locked eyes with Rex.

Rex wagged his tail.

"Yes, about that. I've decided that I am not coming home."

He got three shocked, "Whats!" in reply.

He did his best to explain. "When I set off, I had a route in my head. I was going to go to this place and then to that place. Selina remembers because she helped me plan and book it."

"I did, dad, but it's nearly winter now. Surely you're not proposing to start again."

Albert smiled down at his dog and scratched his ears.

"No, no. I suppose I might try to visit some of the places I missed another time, but you see I was supposed to go around in a big circle, up the country, into Scotland, back down into England, across to Wales, through the home counties and back to East Malling. Catching a ride home now feels like cheating." He looked up to meet his children's faces. "I got talking to one of the chaps who was rescued yesterday and asked him why the earl had him kidnapped. He makes Dorset Knobs. I've never tried one, have you?"

Albert's kids had never heard of the dish and that settled it. He was going to Lyme Regis to find out what they were all about. From there he would find his own way home. He promised.

The End

Author's Notes:

Dear Reader,

Thank you for selecting this book. I hope you enjoyed it, but more than that I hope you read the previous thirteen books in this series so that this one made sense. I bring back a whole host of characters from the previous stories as I am certain you would have noticed if this series is familiar to you.

There's a bunch of items on my list to explain this time around. I'll start with the setting. The village of Glan-Y-Wern was nothing more than a random spot on the map I selected because I needed somewhere remote in Wales. I was writing book four or five when I decided the story had to end there.

Of course, anyone who cares to look at a map or comes from the part of Wales where this is set, will be desperate to point out that Glan-Y-Wern is not on the coast. This would be an easy thing for me to fix; I could just pick a made up name and change it in this and the previous book where it is first mentioned. To do that though would mess with all the people who read *Cornish Pasty Conspiracy – The Killing in the Filling* and presumably that means you.

So I'll put it down to artistic licence and leave it at that.

The name of the bed and breakfast cottage in which Albert stays in this story is a thing from my past. Back in the seventies, my parents would take us to a resort on the coast for a holiday each summer. For a week or two, I don't know which it was, the single digit version of me would leap from sand dunes and build castles with my father.

One year, the property we stayed in, or it might have been the property next door, was called Thistle-Do-Me. Randomly it stuck with me for most of five decades and popped into my head when I needed to give the place in this book a name.

There is a passage where I talk about Albert's arms being numb from the elbow up and his need to climb into a lukewarm bath that still feels hot to his frozen skin. I have experienced this several times in my life; my core temperature dropping to a point where hypothermia and death are knocking on the door.

The first occasion was early in my army career when I endured a weekend exercise called 'Sweet Nut'. We renamed it something else. Returning from it, I had to warm my body over several hours and didn't regain full feeling in my hands for days.

Rex eats his body weight when he finds himself locked in the Gastrothief's cold store. I've had dogs who did this, usually when they find their way into the store where their food is kept. My Labrador, Kira, did this on my wedding day and looks like a blimp in the photographs.

I mention leeks in reference to Welsh food so for those who do not know, the leek is the national emblem of Wales. It comes from an historic battle several centuries ago where the soldiers wore leeks to distinguish themselves from the enemy. The leek can be found displayed all over the place in Wales.

I also employ an explosive called detonation cord or det cord. I didn't make it up - it's a real thing. I first came across it in the army, but it is in common use in the construction industries. Quite how Gloria might have come by some I'll leave to your imagination, she's that kind of woman.

Finishing this little note to the readers, it's a drizzly day in January and I find myself perched on a barstool in my kitchen. My two-year-old forced my wife from bed at 0200hrs this morning, the second day in a row, and we are all tired, my wife more than anyone.

I need to wrap this up now as the next book is waiting and it won't write itself.

Take care.

Steve Higgs

What's Next for Albert and Rex?

Lyme Regis Layover

On their way home, Rex and Albert make one last stop, a quick layover in Lyme Regis.

However, before they can a bite to eat, Rex's powerful nose detects the smell of blood in the air and everything goes south from there.

Albert might want to ignore it, but this time it's personal - the victim is someone he knows.

To order this book, type the link below into your browser.

https://mybook.to/lymeregis

Felicity Philips Investigates

Marriage? It can be absolute murder.

Wedding planner for the rich and famous, Felicity Philips is aiming to land the biggest gig of her life – the next royal wedding. But there are a few obstacles in her way ...

... not least of which is a dead body the police believe she is responsible for murdering.

Out of custody, but under suspicion, her rivals are lining up to ruin her name. With so much on the line, she needs to prove it wasn't her and fast. But that means finding out who the real killer is ...

... without said killer finding out what she is up to.

With Buster the bulldog as her protector and Amber the ragdoll cat providing sartorial wit – mostly aimed at the dog - Felicity is turning sleuth.

What does a wedding planner know about solving a crime?

Nothing. Absolutely nothing.

Pets Investigate

Sticking their noses where they are most definitely not wanted.

Despairing of their humans, these pets take it upon themselves to solve the cases they see as only cats and dogs can.

Whether they sniff out the clues or fool the criminals into thinking they are harmless pets to be ignored, Rex, Amber, Buster, and more enjoy escapades a-plenty in this fun collection of short stories.

Grab your copy and be ready for the fur to fly!

More Books By Steve Higgs

About the Author

At school, the author was mostly disinterested in every subject except creative writing, for which, at age ten, he won his first award. However, calling it his first award suggests that there have been more, which there have not. Accolades may come but, in the meantime, he is having a ball writing mystery stories and crime thrillers and claims to have more than a hundred books forming an unruly queue in his head as they clamour to get out. He lives in the south-east corner of England with a duo of lazy sausage dogs. Surrounded by rolling hills, brooding castles, and vineyards, he doubts he will ever leave, the beer is just too good.

If you are a social media fan, you should copy the link below into your browser to join my very active Facebook group. You'll find a host of friends waiting there, some of whom have been with me from the very start.

My Facebook group get first notification when I publish anything new, plus cover reveals and free short stories, but more than that, they all interact with each other, sharing inside jokes, and answering question.

f facebook.com/stevehiggsauthor

You can also keep updated with my books via my website:

g https://stevehiggsbooks.com/

Made in the USA
Columbia, SC
23 January 2024

30865048R00146